First Came
the Frightening Dream . . .

Mayra was standing on the shore of the lake. The water was light blue, the same color as the sky. Suddenly she stepped into the lake. She didn't sink. She started to walk.

She was walking on the surface of the blue, blue water, looking up at the blue sky, not at all surprised that she could walk over the water.

She took a few steps, then a few steps more. The water felt so cold under her bare feet.

Suddenly she had the feeling that she was being watched. Someone was watching her from the shore. Who was there? Who was watching?

When would she wake up?

FEAR STREET™

the Sleepwalker

R.L. STINE

AN ARCHWAY PAPERBACK
Published by POCKET BOOKS
New York   London   Toronto   Sydney   Tokyo   Singapore

AN ARCHWAY PAPERBACK *Original*

An Archway Paperback published by
POCKET BOOKS, a division of Simon & Schuster Inc.
1230 Avenue of the Americas, New York, NY 10020

ISBN: 0-671-69412-X

First Archway Paperback printing May 1990

10 9 8 7 6 5 4 3 2

Fear Street is a trademark of Parachute Press, Inc.

AN ARCHWAY PAPERBACK and colophon are
registered trademarks of Simon & Schuster Inc.

Printed in the U.S.A.

IL 6+

prologue

As pale as moonlight, Mayra seemed to float across the lawn. Her long coppery hair billowed in the gusting night breeze. Her silky white nightgown shimmered in the soft light, flapping soundlessly in the wind.

Eyes gently closed, Mayra moved effortlessly, almost ghostlike, barefoot over the tall grass.

A chorus of tree toads began to chirp, but the noise didn't stir her. A few seconds later the song ended as abruptly as it had begun. Now the only sound was that of her breathing, hard and irregular, the only sign that she was alive, that she was real and not a beautiful moonlit apparition.

She reached the low hedge at the end of the lawn and turned as if guided by some inner radar. A car turned onto the street and rolled quickly past. The sleepy driver didn't even see her.

Hidden in the shifting night shadows, Mayra floated the length of the hedge. With her long, flowing red hair, her pale white skin, the soft, almost luminous nightgown billowing around her, she looked like a figure from a painting, one of those large Victorian portraits that hang in museums.

When she finally opened her eyes, she didn't know where she was.

She looked down first and saw that her feet were wet from the heavy summer dew. Despite the warmth of the night, she felt chilled all over.

I'm in my nightgown, she realized. And then: I'm outside.

But where outside?

I was having the strangest dream.

The house suddenly loomed up in front of her, as if it, too, could float across the grass.

I'm in my front yard. In my nightgown.

Wisps of black clouds traced over the full moon. The shadows around her suddenly faded and moved.

She realized she was cold, cold not from the air but from fright.

She stared up at her house. It looked so different, so big and unfriendly. The windows were dark. No one was awake inside.

No one knew she was out here, standing in the cold, wet grass.

How did I get out here? Am I awake or asleep?

What is happening to me?

chapter

1

One Week Earlier

Mrs. Barnes yawned as she set the plate of scrambled eggs down in front of Mayra. "Goodness. I wake up more tired than when I go to bed." She was wearing her white nurse's uniform. Mayra noticed that the seams on her mother's white stockings were crooked.

Mayra looked down at the soggy yellow pile on the plate and made a face. "Why do I have to have scrambled eggs so early in the morning?"

"It looks like puke," Mayra's sister, Kim, said with the typical directness of a ten-year-old.

"Don't say things like that at the table," Mrs. Barnes said, yawning again. "Even if they're true."

"But that's what it looks like," Kim protested. "Why can't I say it?" Kim was wearing red short-shorts and a plain white T-shirt, ready for day camp.

"You need a big breakfast," Mrs. Barnes told Mayra, ignoring her younger daughter. "You're starting a new job this morning. You'll need plenty of energy."

"A little cholesterol to get me going. Thank you, Nurse Nancy," Mayra said, reluctantly poking her fork in the eggs.

"Nurse Nancy. Nurse Nancy," Kim repeated. For some reason it struck her funny.

Having a mother who was a nurse had certain drawbacks, Mayra thought. One of the major drawbacks was all the healthy food you were forced to eat.

Mrs. Barnes took a sip of coffee. "Oh, no. Wouldn't you know it?" A small brown splash of coffee stained her white uniform. She rushed to the sink to get a wet cloth to wash the stain off.

Mayra poured about a pound and a half of salt on the eggs, and they didn't taste too bad. "I can't believe I'm going to work today," she grumbled. "Some summer!"

"Some summer. Some summer," Kim mimicked, her mouth full of cornflakes.

"Stop repeating everything I say," Mayra snapped at her.

In retaliation, Kim opened her mouth wide, showing Mayra the wad of chewed-up cereal inside.

"I can't believe you got the job at all," Mrs. Barnes said, returning to the table with a big wet spot on her uniform breast.

"Hey—thanks for the vote of confidence!" Mayra said, laughing.

"No. That's not what I meant. I never thought Mrs. Cottler would hire you—because of me." She very carefully took another sip of coffee, holding the saucer under the cup. "I took care of her when she was in the hospital sometime last year. Ooh—what a pain in the you-know-where."

"Where?" Kim asked, then burst out laughing.

"Mrs. Cottler never stopped complaining about the hospital—or about me. Nothing I did seemed to please her. She even called my supervisor in and told her I was a terrible nurse and I was trying to kill her. Can you imagine?"

Mayra couldn't imagine. She knew how hardworking and serious her mother was about her job at the hospital. Ever since her parents had divorced and Mayra's dad had left, the nursing job had been the most important thing in Mrs. Barnes's life—except for Mayra and Kim, of course.

"So when I heard you had applied for a job with Mrs. Cottler, I didn't think you stood a chance," Mayra's mother continued, sipping coffee. "I guess maybe she doesn't realize that you're my daughter."

Mayra dropped her fork. She suddenly had a heavy feeling in the pit of her stomach. "You mean she's a horrible old witch? Why did you let me take this job?"

"I'm sure she'll be very nice to you," her mother said quickly, realizing maybe she shouldn't have told Mayra about Mrs. Cottler's hospital stay. "You said she was nice when she interviewed you."

"Yeah. She was very sweet," Mayra said.

"And she's paying such a generous salary," Mrs. Barnes said, taking her empty cup to the sink and rinsing it out. "I mean, five dollars an hour just to straighten up, prepare her lunch, and read to her in the afternoon? Come on, Mayra—you lucked out."

"I guess," Mayra said, deciding to give up on the eggs. She drank down her glass of orange juice in one gulp.

"No guessing about it. We really can use the money, you know. Your father, wherever he is, isn't contributing a penny." A bitter frown crossed Mrs. Barnes's face, making her look older than her thirty-nine years.

"Why can't I have a job?" Kim asked. There were puddles of milk on the table all around her bowl. Mayra had always been neat and careful. Kim was the opposite of Mayra in just about every way.

"You *do* have a job," Mayra teased. "Being a good little girl."

"You're stupid" was Kim's reply.

A horn honked out on the street.

"That's your day-camp bus," Mrs. Barnes cried, running to the front door to signal to the driver that Kim would be right out. "Is your camp bag packed? Do you have everything?"

"Yes, Mom," Kim said, grabbing up the canvas bag and heading to the door.

"How about shoes? Don't you think you'll need shoes?" Mrs. Barnes asked, pointing. Kim was leaving for camp barefoot.

A few minutes later Kim was on her way with camp bag—and shoes. Mrs. Barnes returned to the kitchen, where Mayra was rinsing off her plate and glass, having taken advantage of her mother's absence to dump the remainder of her eggs into the garbage disposal.

"I've got to get to the hospital," Mrs. Barnes said, straightening her white stockings. "You all set for your job?"

"Not after what you told me!" Mayra exclaimed, drying her hands. "Mrs. Cottler will probably treat me like a total slave. She'll chain me up and force me to scrub her fireplace with a toothbrush!"

"You and your wild imagination," her mother said, sighing. "I never should've told you that story. I forgot how creative you can be, how you're always exaggerating, making things worse than they are."

"Is that what you think of me?" Mayra asked, a little hurt.

Mrs. Barnes kissed her on the forehead in reply, picked up her bag, and headed toward the front door. "Do you want a lift?"

"No. Thanks. I want to walk. Burn off those eggs."

"Mrs. Cottler lives on Fear Street, doesn't she? You're certainly brave this morning."

"Yeah, she lives back near the lake. But I don't mind Fear Street in the daylight," Mayra said. "I mean, what could happen?"

chapter
2

"Oh! My beads!"

Hazel, Mrs. Cottler's black cat, swiped at Mayra's beads. They broke and clattered over the kitchen floor.

"What happened, Mayra?" Mrs. Cottler called from the dining room.

"Oh, nothing. Just my beads," Mayra said, bending over to retrieve them. The cat, alarmed that Mayra had dived down on all fours, ran out of the room. I loved these beads, Mayra thought. Walker, her new boyfriend, had given them to her the night before he left with his family on vacation. They were glass, pale blue like opals. She had promised him she'd wear them every day and think of him every time she saw them. But now . . .

"Oh. Your beads broke." Mrs. Cottler appeared in the doorway. "Can I help?"

"No. I think I got them all." Mayra climbed to her feet, the beads in her cupped hands.

"Let me restring them for you." Leaning on her cane, Mrs. Cottler held out her hands, which were surprisingly smooth and didn't look like an old lady's hands at all. With her smooth, white skin, dark red lips, and coal black hair, Mrs. Cottler looked much younger than her years. Only the cane gave away her age. She looked very summery and colorful in a long, flower-print skirt and butter yellow blouse.

"No. That's okay. Really," Mayra protested.

"I insist, Mayra. I'd enjoy it. I love stringing beads. Please—give them to me. It's good to keep these old hands busy."

Mayra reluctantly handed the beads over to Mrs. Cottler. The old woman gave her a very pleased smile and started back toward the dining room with them. "Pour out some more soup and come finish lunch with me," she called.

It was Wednesday afternoon, Mayra's third day at Mrs. Cottler's, and to Mayra's relief, the two of them were getting along really well. Mrs. Cottler was moody sometimes, and she had a tendency to repeat herself a lot. But she was constantly complimenting Mayra, telling her how pretty she was, how beautiful her long red hair was when the sunlight caught it, telling her what a pleasant reading voice she had —even complimenting her on the simple lunches she prepared.

"It's just canned chicken noodle soup and a ham and cheese sandwich," Mayra had protested, embarrassed by Mrs. Cottler's extravagant praise.

"The simple things are the best, don't you agree?" the old woman said, giving her a warm smile.

This may turn out to be an easy job after all, Mayra thought, staring out the kitchen window at the lake, surrounded by the lush, green Fear Street woods. Is that someone swimming in the lake? She squinted her eyes to see better. No. There was no one there. Just her imagination. She was always trying to make things more interesting than they were!

After lunch Mrs. Cottler would take a short nap on the living-room couch while Mayra cleaned up the dishes. The nap never lasted more than an hour, but it gave Mayra time to watch TV, to think about Walker, and to explore the house.

The house was furnished with surprisingly modern furniture—black leather and chrome chairs and couch, a low glass coffee table. The walls were lined with floor-to-ceiling bookshelves. Mrs. Cottler loved to read. Now that she was older, reading made her eyes tired, so she loved to be read to.

What amazed Mayra about the house was the astounding collection of knickknacks. They covered the tables and counters and windowsills, were arranged in special glass display cases, and stood beside the books in the bookshelves. Mayra found colorful vases and ancient-looking pieces of sculpture, porcelain figures of strange-looking people, antique jars filled with shells, or feathers, or colorful powders, carved cats and birds of wood and stone, a pair of tiny white gloves stained brown with age, rimless eyeglasses and a monocle, faded, pressed flowers, a ceramic chicken's foot, several carved moon crescents, a stuffed white owl.

Mayra tried to imagine why Mrs. Cottler had kept

some of these things. But it was impossible to figure out why someone would keep a small stuffed mouse on the piano next to a papier-mâché pig's mask and a bronze figurine of a boy with one arm.

"What an amazing collection!" Mayra had exclaimed to Mrs. Cottler on her first day in the house.

The old woman shook her head and chuckled. "Just junk," she said. "Just an old woman's junk collection gathering dust." When Mayra tried to ask her more about it, Mrs. Cottler changed the subject by saying, "It's time for our walk now."

Every afternoon they took a short walk by the lake shore, Mrs. Cottler leaning on her cane with one hand, sometimes holding on to Mayra's arm with the other. Walking such a long distance on the marshy ground was obviously difficult for the old woman. But she insisted they do it without fail every afternoon.

For some reason this became Mayra's least favorite part of the job. She knew she should enjoy the fresh, cool air off the lake, the bright sunshine, the chance to get out of the cluttered, old house. But the daily walks made her feel uncomfortable, on edge, nervous. And as she would stare out over the green blue water, Mayra felt chilled, even on the hottest days.

Now as she helped Mrs. Cottler around a thick clump of weeds that leaned toward the shore, the old woman got a faraway look in her eyes. "Mrs. Cottler —are you okay?"

Staring into the sparkling lake, Mrs. Cottler didn't seem to hear her. "I lost Vincent here," she said softly.

"Vincent?"

"My son. He was only three. He shouldn't have run

from me. He didn't know how to swim." She turned her head from Mayra and sighed. "Sometimes I think I see him out here. All these years later, and I still see him." She gripped Mayra's arm tighter.

"When did it happen?" Mayra asked.

Mrs. Cottler didn't answer. She remained silent for a long while, and then finally turned back toward the house. "Let's go in. It's time to read now."

Nicholas Nickleby by Charles Dickens was the book Mrs. Cottler wanted Mayra to read first. It was a huge brick of a book. Mayra was sure it would take the entire summer to read it. She had been forced to read *Great Expectations* in school that year. It was okay, she thought, but not anything she'd choose to read. She was surprised to find that she was enjoying *Nicholas Nickleby*. It was actually pretty funny.

Mrs. Cottler sat up very straight on the black leather couch as Mayra read, stroking Hazel, who stayed awake at her side as if listening to Mayra read. Sometimes Mrs. Cottler closed her eyes. Mayra wasn't certain if she was just resting them or if she had dozed off, but she continued reading anyway.

It was so quiet in the house. The only sounds were the gentle purring of the black cat, Mayra's voice, and the ticking of the bronze clock above the mantel.

"Mayra, I'm a little chilled." Mrs. Cottler's interruption startled Mayra. She thought the old woman was asleep. "Would you run upstairs and bring down a sweater from my dresser?"

"Yes, of course," Mayra said, closing the book and getting up quickly.

"It's so hard for me to get up and down the stairs these days," Mrs. Cottler said. She had already said it three or four times that afternoon. "It's my legs. I'm in pretty good shape except for these old legs."

Yes, you're in great shape, Mayra thought as she hurried up the stairs. She has such amazing skin. Her face is as smooth as mine. How does she do it?

Mayra walked through the dark hallway to Mrs. Cottler's bedroom at the end of the hall. She looked around. The room had dark blue wallpaper with tiny white stars that seemed to twinkle. There were two dressers across from the queen-size bed, side by side against the far wall.

Which dresser had the sweaters?

Mayra picked the dresser on the right and pulled open the top drawer. "Wow!" How strange. The drawer was filled with black candles, dozens of long black candles.

Mayra reached in and picked one up. She sniffed it, surprised by its sour scent. It smelled old, musty. The wax felt smooth and hard in Mayra's hand. And the wick was as black as the candle wax.

What weird candles, Mayra thought, picking up another one. Why did Mrs. Cottler have black candles? And why did she keep them hidden away in a dresser drawer?

A loud shriek behind her made Mayra drop both candles.

Her heart pounding, she turned to find Hazel, the black cat, staring at her, green eyes aglow.

"Okay, okay, Hazel. No need to make such a racket. I'm coming."

Mayra replaced the black candles in the dresser drawer, found a sweater in the drawer below it, and hurried to bring it downstairs to Mrs. Cottler. All the while she could feel the cat's eyes on her, admonishing her for looking where she shouldn't have looked, accusing her, warning her. . . .

chapter
3

Mayra said goodbye to Mrs. Cottler and stepped outside, closing the heavy front door behind her. She took a deep breath of fresh air and looked up at the sky. Heavy, dark clouds covered the sun. I'd better get home before it starts to rain, she thought.

She adjusted her Walkman, tuned it to Q-100, the station that played the best music, and started down the flagstone walk to the street. She couldn't get the black cat out of her mind, the way it shrieked at her when it saw her holding the black candles, the way it stared at her. Stop, Mayra. Just stop, she scolded herself. You're letting your imagination run away with you once again. She walked faster, letting the loud music in her ears sweep away all of her thoughts.

"Just think about how much money you'll have at the end of summer," she told herself. "Think about how you'll be able to buy new clothes before school starts and not feel guilty about it."

She drifted with the music, walking in rhythm to it, not thinking about anything, starting to feel good, letting the insistent pounding of the synthesized drums carry her along the street.

For some reason her father's face flashed into her mind. How long had it been since she'd seen him? Over a year. She wondered if he had changed, if he looked different. Why hadn't she heard from him? "Because he doesn't care," she told herself. "Because he doesn't care about any of us. That's why he left."

She scolded herself again for exaggerating.

She forced herself to think about something pleasant. Walker. She realized she missed her new boyfriend a lot. He was away for two weeks. Two whole weeks. She remembered the night before he left. Those long, long kisses . . .

She drifted back into the music, turning up the volume. The louder the music, the less chance of troublesome thoughts entering her mind. "Go with the flow," she said aloud. "Go with it. Just go with it."

She was about to turn onto Fear Street when a hand grabbed her shoulder.

"Oh!"

Startled, she pulled the headphones off and spun around. "Link! Why'd you grab me like that?"

He grinned. "I've been calling to you for half a block."

"Oh. I guess I had the radio too loud." She reached down and clicked off the Walkman. "Well, what are you doing here, Link?"

His dark eyes playfully stared into hers. He tossed back his wavy, black hair. He was wearing faded jean cutoffs and a sleeveless blue T-shirt. Even though summer was just beginning, he already had a tan.

Okay, okay. So he's real good-looking, Mayra thought to herself. The problem is, he knows it.

"I—I just wanted to talk to you, Mayra."

"I don't think so, Link. I really don't want to talk to you." She turned and started walking. She couldn't believe she was being this cold, this mean to him—but what choice did she have? She had broken up with him a month earlier, and here he was, still following her around like a sad little puppy dog.

"I think we've said everything there is to be said," she added without turning around.

He ran to catch up with her. He grabbed her arm. "I don't think so. I still have more to say."

"Write me a letter," she snapped. Wow, she even surprised *herself* with that one!

She pulled her arm out of his grasp. "Let go, Link. Look. I'm sorry. I don't want to be mean to you. But it's over. I'm going with Walker now. You've got to leave me alone."

"But, Mayra—" He flashed her his pleading look, the one that used to melt her heart every time. Now she thought he just looked silly.

How could I have cared so much about him? she asked herself. He's so—superficial.

"If we could just sit down somewhere and talk for a few minutes, I'm sure we could straighten everything out," Link said, running in front of her to block her path.

He's so much like his sister, Stephanie, Mayra suddenly thought. The two of them could be twins.

They're both so dark and good-looking, both so energetic. They both talk so fast, move so fast, always seem to be speeded up, always seem to be excited about something.

"There's nothing to straighten out. Just let it drop," Mayra said, sounding as exasperated as she felt. Since she'd broken up with him, he'd been bombarding her with phone calls, following her everywhere.

"Look, Link, I've been working all day. I'm tired and I want to get home before it rains."

"But you and me—that's much more important than a little rain," he said, walking backward, staying in front of her.

He's so conceited, she thought. He should go out with himself!

"There's no more you and me. I told you—I'm going with Walker."

"He's a dweeb."

"A what? Look, *you're* the dweeb. Don't start calling him babyish names. Now get out of my way and let me get home!"

He obediently stopped and stepped aside. She hurried past him. "But, Mayra, if you'd just give me a chance—" he called after her.

"Have a nice life!" she screamed, and started to run.

"You'll be sorry!" he yelled, more sad than angry. "You'll be sorry, Mayra!"

When she turned around, he was gone.

chapter
4

"Now, settle yourself, Hazel," Mrs. Cottler said, leaning down to the cat. "Mayra's going to read to us."

The old woman smiled as the cat obediently hopped up onto the couch beside her. "Do begin, Mayra. I'm so much enjoying this book, largely because of your excellent reading of it."

"Thank you, Mrs. Cottler." Mayra opened the book and shuffled through the pages until she found chapter four. Before she could begin reading, there was a loud knock at the door.

"Now, who could that be?" Mrs. Cottler asked, leaning on her cane as she struggled to her feet. The knock repeated, a little louder. "Hold your horses. We're coming."

Mayra got to the door first and pulled it open. A balding, middle-aged man with a red face glared at her angrily. Despite the heat of the afternoon sun, he was wearing a charcoal gray wool suit. He mopped his broad forehead with an already wet handkerchief. Mayra saw that he was carrying a peach in his other hand.

"Where's Mrs. Cottler?" he demanded without saying hello or giving Mayra any kind of greeting.

"I'm coming, I'm coming," Mrs. Cottler called from behind Mayra. "Is that you again, Mr. Clean?"

"It's Kleeg—not Clean!" he shouted angrily. His face got even redder.

"What do you want this time, Mr. Clean?" Mrs. Cottler asked, appearing beside Mayra in the doorway.

He rolled his eyes and held up the peach. "What do *you* think?" he asked nastily.

"Oh, not the peaches again. I already told you, there's nothing I can do about that."

Mayra took a step back. Mr. Clean or Kleeg, or whoever he was, was looking more and more unpleasant.

"You *have* to do something about it!" he said. "I've asked you six times. I'm not asking anymore. The peaches from your tree fall all over my backyard."

"Well, enjoy them," Mrs. Cottler snapped. "Mayra, close the door."

"I can't mow my lawn! I can't walk in my yard because of your peaches!" the neighbor screamed.

"I can't make the peaches stay up in the tree," Mrs. Cottler said. Mayra saw that her eyes were glowing. She's really enjoying this, Mayra realized.

Mr. Kleeg turned and stepped off the front porch. "I'm going to cut down the tree. That's what I'm going to do." He heaved the peach angrily. It bounced off the frame of the screen door.

"Calm down, Mr. Clean," Mrs. Cottler warned gently. "You're not going to do anything of the kind. Don't get so worked up in this heat. Something terrible could happen to you."

He cursed loudly and stormed off in the direction of his house.

"Oh, that man. What a nuisance," Mrs. Cottler muttered, more to herself than to Mayra. "What a nuisance." She turned to Mayra and smiled. "Close the door, please."

Mayra started to close the door, then stopped. "Oh, look. He dropped his handkerchief," she said. She opened the screen door, bent down, and picked it up off the porch floor. "Should I run and return it to him?"

Mrs. Cottler's eyes lit up and her dark lips formed a very pleased smile. "No. No, dear. Don't return it to him. Hand it to me."

She grabbed the damp handkerchief from Mayra's hand, and tucked it into the pocket of her skirt. Then she headed back to the couch. "If he wants it, he can come get it. Now let's read our chapter."

As Mayra began to read, her mind wandered. She thought about Walker. He'd be back from vacation on Saturday. She wondered if he was thinking of her. Maybe right at this very moment.

She tried to send out a mental signal to him as she continued to read the tiny type. She formed a picture of him in her mind—his short blond hair, his blue eyes, his shy smile.

I'm thinking of you, Walker. I'm thinking of you. Are you thinking of me?

He'd be proud of me, she thought. Walker was very

serious about magic. He wanted to be a professional magician. And he was into mental telepathy and psychic powers.

Mayra had never thought much about that stuff. But in the few weeks they had been seeing each other, Walker had taught her a lot. He'd be pleased to know that I'm trying to communicate with him this way, she thought.

Suddenly she realized that Mrs. Cottler was talking to her. "What? I'm sorry," Mayra said. "I was so caught up in the book, I didn't hear you."

"That's okay. You're reading so beautifully," Mrs. Cottler said, stroking Hazel. "I'm glad you're enjoying it too." She started to get up. "But I'm feeling tired this afternoon. I guess it's the heat. Would you be so kind as to help me up the stairs to my room?"

"Of course," Mayra said, putting down the book and hurrying over to give the old woman a hand.

"You can go home early. I'm going to take a nap."

Mayra helped Mrs. Cottler up the stairs and down the hall into the bedroom. She said goodbye and went back downstairs, thinking again of Walker, wondering if he had gotten her mental message. She hoisted the heavy book back onto the shelf and, preparing to leave, noticed Mrs. Cottler's cane on the floor in front of the couch.

"I'd better take it up for her," Mayra told herself.

She was almost to the top of the stairs with the cane when Hazel appeared above her on the landing. The cat's yellow green eyes flared. She arched her back and hissed at Mayra.

"Hazel, what's wrong with you?" Mayra scolded. "Why do you keep doing that? It's only me." She climbed another few steps. The cat stared down at her, with her back still arched. "How quickly they forget," Mayra said. "We're friends, remember?"

The cat hissed menacingly in reply.

It's almost as if she doesn't want me to come upstairs, Mayra thought. But then she realized that was silly. Just because she's a black cat, you don't have to start imagining that she's different from other cats, Mayra scolded herself. She's probably hissing at a bug, or at a mouse, or at nothing at all.

She brushed past Hazel, who stared up at her, looking surprised that Mayra had dared to challenge her. She carried the cane to Mrs. Cottler's room.

The door was half open. The room was dark except for a narrow rectangle of light from the window. Mrs. Cottler sat up stiffly on her bed facing the wall. Her eyes seemed to be closed.

Mayra hesitated at the doorway. "Mrs. Cottler?" she called softly.

The old woman didn't answer.

Mayra saw that she had Mr. Kleeg's white handkerchief in her hand. "Mrs. Cottler?"

Again no reply.

Is she in a trance or something? Mayra wondered. What is she doing?

She took a step into the room. The cat suddenly rubbed against her legs, startling her. The room felt cold, much colder than the hallway.

Mrs. Cottler didn't move.

I'd better get out of here, Mayra thought.

She propped the cane up against the wall and ran down the stairs without looking back.

chapter

5

"Mayra, you really think she's a witch?"

"Well, she has a black cat. And her house is filled with all sorts of strange things, animal feet and stuff. And she has a drawer full of black candles hidden in her bedroom. And she was sitting on her bed in some kind of a trance—at least, she looked like she was in a trance—holding that man's handkerchief. What would *you* think?"

"I would think that you have a very vivid imagination!"

Mayra was in her room, brushing her hair as she talked on the phone to her best friend, Donna Cash. It was Friday morning, a few minutes before she had to leave for work.

"There's got to be a logical explanation here," Donna said.

"Sure, there's a logical explanation, Donna. Mrs. Cottler is a witch!"

24

"Well," Donna said thoughtfully, "I really don't believe it. Why don't you just ask her?"

"What do I say? 'Are you a witch, Mrs. Cottler?' That's kind of personal, isn't it, Donna?"

"I guess."

"Besides, I'm not supposed to know about the black candles or anything. And she'd probably freak if she knew I saw her in that trance."

"I guess."

"Mrs. Cottler is always so nice to me," Mayra said. "It's hard to believe that—"

"You'd just better stay on her good side," Donna said.

"Yeah. You're probably right."

"Hey—I was only joking. Come on, Mayra, lighten up. You don't really believe that people can cast spells on other people, do you?"

"I just kept remembering something Link's sister, Stephanie, told us," Mayra said, dropping the hairbrush, not bothering to pick it up. "Remember, she was always taking out those weird books on the occult from the library?"

"Yeah. Stephanie was really into that for a while. I think it was before she discovered sex!" Donna laughed. She was a tiny girl, shortest in the class, but she had a raucous laugh.

"Well, we were over at Stephanie's one day and—"

"And you were probably coming on to Link—right?"

"Give me a break, Donna! Stephanie was reading to us from this book on witchcraft. And it said that in order to cast a spell, a witch needs an item of clothing or a belonging of the victim's. And I remembered the happy look on Mrs. Cottler's face when that poor man left his handkerchief behind. And then there she was, holding it so tightly with her eyes closed and—"

"Whoa! Slow down, Mayra," Donna interrupted. Then Mayra heard her yell to her mother, "I'm getting off the phone! Just give me one second!"

"I've got to get off too," Mayra said, glancing at the clock.

"Well, you sound too serious about this witchcraft stuff," Donna said. "It's all just a crock, Mayra. Your problem is, you've been hanging out with Walker too much."

"Now, what's that supposed to mean?" Mayra snapped. She hadn't meant to sound so angry.

"Nothing. It's just that he believes all that mystical magic stuff, and now you do too."

"You don't like Walker, do you?" Mayra asked accusingly.

"I didn't say that. Walker's okay. He's just weird, that's all."

"You think he's weird because he's interested in something," Mayra said, surprising herself at how angry she felt. "He's not like all the other boys at school who just like to party and mess around. He has an ambition. He's serious about something."

"He's pretty cute too," Donna said, obviously trying to keep it light.

"I'm sorry," Mayra said quickly. "I didn't mean to give you a hard time. I guess I'm just nervous about Mrs. Cottler and about seeing Walker Sunday night for the first time in two weeks."

"Yeah, you sounded pretty intense. But that's okay."

"Well, I know kids at school think Walker is strange because he's into magic. And because he's really shy. But I don't want my best friend to think he's strange too."

"I don't," Donna said. "I mean, I don't really know him that well. *Okay, okay! I'm getting off the phone!* Hey, speaking of Stephanie, have you seen her since you broke up with Link?"

"No. Not really. Once, I guess. As soon as school ended, she started a summer job too. She's an assistant in a day-care center, or something."

"But she's home at nights, right? She could have called you."

"Donna, you're a troublemaker."

"What are friends for?"

"You think Stephanie is mad at me because I broke up with her brother?"

"I dunno."

"Well, thanks for planting the idea in my mind. I needed something else to worry about. I gotta go."

"Me too. Give Walker a big kiss for me Sunday."

"Donna, get your own boyfriend. Get a life. Get *something.*"

"Get lost!"

Both girls laughed and hung up the phone.

It's nice to have such a secure friendship, Mayra thought. Donna and I can say whatever we're really thinking to each other, and know that it won't damage our feelings for each other.

However, she did wish that Donna hadn't reminded her about Stephanie. Stephanie and Link were so close. It was very unusual. They didn't fight or compete like other brothers and sisters. Even though Stephanie was nearly Link's age, she really looked up to her brother, worshiped him even.

Donna's probably right, Mayra thought as she took one last look at herself in the mirror, straightened the shoulder strings of her green-and-white sundress, and headed down the stairs. Stephanie is probably furious at me for dumping her brother. That's why she hasn't called all summer.

Oh, well, she thought with genuine sadness, I guess I lost a good friend as well as a boyfriend. . . .

Mayra saw the ambulance as she turned the corner onto Fear Street.

"Oh, no! Mrs. Cottler!" she cried aloud, and started to run across the neighbors' lawns to the house. But as she came closer, she realized that the ambulance wasn't parked in front of Mrs. Cottler's. It was parked in front of the house next door.

She stopped in Mrs. Cottler's driveway and watched as two tall paramedics dressed in white carried a stretcher down the walk to the ambulance. Covered up to his chin by a white blanket, the man lying on the stretcher groaned in pain, his eyes shut tight. Mayra recognized him at once. It was Mr. Kleeg.

The paramedics slid the stretcher into the back of the ambulance and secured the doors. A few seconds later the ambulance pulled away from the curb, its red light flashing, reflecting against the green tree leaves overhead.

Mayra looked up toward Mrs. Cottler's house. There was the old woman standing behind the screen door, Hazel in her arms. She had been watching the whole scene.

"Mrs. Cottler, what happened?" Mayra called, jogging up to the porch.

Mrs. Cottler had an excited smile on her face. But as Mayra approached, she changed her expression to a more somber one. "Poor Mr. Clean," she said, holding open the screen door for Mayra. "What an awful, awful thing."

"But—what? What happened?" Mayra cried, out of breath.

"Poor Mr. Clean," Mrs. Cottler repeated. "He fell and broke his hip. Oh, that must be painful." She shook her head. "I warned him something bad would happen the way he was carrying on yesterday. Oh, that poor, poor man."

chapter
6

Walker greeted her shyly, stepping out of the front door to his house, giving her a nervous half smile and reaching out his hand to shake hers. He was wearing jeans with holes at the knees and a Phoenix Suns T-shirt, which he'd probably picked up on his vacation.

She laughed. He looked so stiff and awkward trying to shake hands with her. She dodged around his hand, hopped up on tiptoes, and kissed him quickly on the cheek.

She loved the way he blushed. Just two pink circles on his white cheeks.

"Hey, you've been traveling out West for two weeks. How come you don't have a tan?" she asked, taking his arm and guiding him to the front yard.

"I don't know," he said, shrugging. "I guess maybe if we'd stopped driving and stepped out of the car for three minutes, I might have gotten some sun."

"Where did you go? I only got one postcard from you. The one with the cactus."

He sighed and shook his head. "It was incredible. We went everywhere. We drove the southern route out, then came back by the northern route. The desert was the most beautiful part. It just stretched on forever, so flat and white, like a gigantic ocean."

"Did you go to the Grand Canyon?"

"Yeah. I think I hypnotized one of the mules there."

She laughed and pulled him down onto the grass beside her. "You were practicing your hypnotism?"

He looked embarrassed. "A little. The mule didn't want to go down the canyon, so I did a little hocus-pocus."

"You're joking."

"Yes, I am," he said, and laughed.

I love his laugh, she thought. He laughs so seldom. He's usually so serious, but he looks so cute when he laughs.

She took his hand, surprised at how cold it was. He's nervous too, she thought. For some reason it made her feel good. "You have the biggest hands," she said. She pressed her palm against his, spreading her fingers against his. "Look." His fingers were nearly two inches longer.

"Big hands are good for magic," he said. "I can palm a rabbit." He pulled his hand away and reached into his pocket. "Show you a new card trick." He always had a deck of cards in his back jeans pocket.

"Card tricks are dorky," she said. It was okay. It wasn't the first time she had told him that.

"Yeah, I know." He grinned and held up the deck. "Pick a card."

He showed her *three* new card tricks. She tried really hard, but she couldn't figure out how he did them. He really was a good magician, she decided. He really had talent.

He removed a quarter from his pocket. "Let me show you some close-up magic I practiced in the car."

"Why don't you show me some pizza instead?" she asked, standing up and trying to pull him up off the grass. He was so long and lanky. She felt as if she were trying to pick up a giant!

"Pizza? I don't know that trick."

"I'm starving!" she cried. She gave his hand another tug and he came up, pulling her off-balance and almost knocking her over.

"Oh. Sorry." The two pink spots appeared on his pale cheeks.

She reached up both hands, pulled down his head, and kissed him on the lips. "Glad to see you," she said, looking into his ocean blue eyes.

She was disappointed that he looked so uncomfortable.

He seemed to loosen up a bit at Ray's Pizza Place in the Division Street Mall. "I like your sundress," he said, wiping cheese off his chin with a paper napkin. "I-I've never seen your shoulders before."

"I have two of them," she said.

"I know. I counted."

The waitress brought their Cokes.

"Hey—where are the beads?" he asked.

"What?"

"The beads I gave you."

Mayra automatically reached for them around her neck, but of course they weren't there. "Mrs. Cottler has them. Her cat broke them, and she's going to restring them for me." She may have forgotten about them. I'd better remind her, Mayra thought.

"I'll show you a trick with this straw," Walker said, changing the subject. He twirled the straw easily between his fingers until it completely disappeared.

"How'd you do that?" she asked.

He opened his other hand. The straw was in it, folded in half. "How'd you do it?" she repeated.

He raised a long finger to his lips. "Ssshh. I can't reveal that."

"Well, then, tell me more about your vacation." She took a big bite of pizza and tomato sauce squirted across the table.

"How'd you do *that?*" he joked.

"It's magic," she said, her mouth full.

"There's nothing much to tell about the vacation. I was with my parents, remember?"

"Did you fight with your dad about your magic?"

"A little. He was pretty good, though. I mean, he still thinks I should be a lawyer who does magic tricks on the side. But he didn't bring it up too often. Only every two hundred miles or so."

"And your mom?"

"She was busy pointing out each and every horse or cactus. I had to keep reminding her that I'm sixteen, not six!"

She took his hand in hers. "I'm glad you're back."

As they walked out of the restaurant and into the brightly lit mall, Walker started to look uncomfortable again. "You know, Mayra, I'm really sorry about last time."

"What?"

"Our last date. I've been wanting to apologize."

Mayra was very confused. She looked up at him, trying to read his thoughts. What was there to apologize about? All she remembered were the kisses, the long, tender kisses. It was a wonderful night, she remembered. She had felt so close to him that night. She had even wished that he hadn't been so shy, that he had wanted to go further than just kisses.

Such thoughts.

"Apologize for what?" she asked. "It was a really nice night."

He seemed very pleased, even relieved by this answer. "Well, okay. It's just that I got you home so late, I was worried that maybe you got into trouble." He put his arm around her shoulder, and they continued walking happily through the nearly empty mall.

"Mom—you're still up?" Mayra was startled to see her mother in the leather armchair in the living room. The room was dark except for the hall light behind them.

"Oh. Uh—hi!" Mrs. Barnes shook herself awake and stood up quickly. She was still wearing her white nurse's uniform. "I guess I fell asleep in the chair. I got home about two hours ago."

"Well, why didn't you go to bed?" Mayra asked, yawning.

"I didn't think I was tired." She stretched. "Now I *know* I'm tired. Did you have a good time with Walker?"

"Yeah. Fine." Mayra never talked much about Walker to her mother. She wasn't sure how her mother felt about him. She was always praising Link to the sky, telling Mayra what a "nice boy" he was. When Mayra broke up with Link, her mother tried but didn't succeed in hiding her disappointment. She had never offered an opinion about Walker.

"Did he enjoy his vacation out West?"

"Yeah. I guess it was great. They went everywhere." Mayra yawned again. "And he got to practice his magic a lot in the car."

Mrs. Barnes shook her head. "He certainly is devoted to his magic."

Mayra couldn't tell how her mother meant that. But she was too tired to get into it. "Guess I'll go to bed. You working tomorrow?"

"Yeah. Early morning shift. I've got to leave in a few hours, believe it or not. You go on up. I'll close up."

Her mother suddenly looked a lot older to Mayra. Or maybe it was just the harsh hall light. Mayra said good night and started up the stairs.

"Oh, I almost forgot—" That was one of her mother's most irritating habits, Mayra realized. She always remembered something when you were halfway up the stairs, and you had to turn around and go back down to hear what it was. "Link called about an hour and a half ago."

"Link? Oh, brother." Mayra made a face. "What did you tell him?"

"I told him you weren't here. It seemed like the right thing to say—especially since you weren't here."

That was her mother's idea of a joke.

"He doesn't give up," Mayra muttered. To her surprise, she realized she was a little bit flattered. Link really isn't such a bad guy, she thought. Sometimes things just don't work out, that's all. . . .

She called good night to her mother again and, thinking about Link, headed up to her room.

That night was the night she had the dream for the first time.

In the dream she was standing on the shore of the lake. The water was light blue, the same color as the sky. She was surrounded by blue. Suddenly she stepped into the lake. She didn't sink. She started to walk. She was walking on the surface of the blue, blue water, looking up at the blue sky, not at all surprised that she could walk over the water.

She took a few steps, then a few steps more. The water felt so cold under her bare feet.

Suddenly she had the feeling that she was being watched. Someone was watching her from the shore. It made her feel uncomfortable. Who was there? Who was watching?

She tried to see, but she couldn't. Feeling very uncomfortable, very unhappy, she took another step across the lake, then another. It became very windy. Her clothing was blowing all around her. The lake water lapped up over her ankles.

Who was there? Who was watching her?

Mayra opened her eyes and found herself surrounded by darkness.

This wasn't the darkness of her bedroom.

She was awake now. The dream was over.

So why didn't her bedroom come back into focus?

Her bare feet were so cold, so wet. She looked down and saw that she was standing in tall, wet grass. Her nightgown fluttered around her in the wind. The front of her house loomed above her like a silent, giant creature.

Where am I?

How did I get here?

She wrapped her arms around herself and stared up at the house. Was this her house? Why did it look so different?

It's so dark, so cold and so dark.

Why am I standing here?

The trees whispered and swayed. The ground seemed to tilt. She held her arms out to steady herself.

Then she saw that the front door was wide open.

Did I walk here? Did I walk out here in my sleep?

Something is wrong, Mayra thought. *Something is horribly wrong.*

chapter

7

"*D*elicious lunch, Mayra."

"Thank you, Mrs. Cottler."

Sunlight filtered through the curtains in the window above the kitchen sink as Mayra hurried to finish washing the dishes. She was eager to get their daily walk by the lake out of the way and begin reading to Mrs. Cottler. Maybe the book would help take her mind off the frightening sleepwalking episode of the night before.

If only she'd been able to tell someone about it. Talking about it would probably make it seem less frightening to her. But her mother had already gone to work. She had called Walker's house first thing in the morning, but his mother said he wasn't up yet. Donna had already left for work. So there was no one to tell.

Had she really walked in her sleep? Walked down the front stairs, unlocked the front door, and crossed the front yard almost to the street with her eyes closed and her arms outstretched like someone in a horror movie?

Mayra had so many questions she needed to have answered. She had never sleepwalked before. Why had she done it last night? Where was she going? What would have happened if she hadn't awakened? Would she have kept right on walking?

The dream was just as troubling as the sleepwalking. She ran it through her mind again and again. It didn't make any sense to her. Why was she walking across the lake? To meet someone? To get away from someone? And who was watching her from the shore?

Did the dream cause her to sleepwalk? Was there a connection between the two?

She just *had* to talk to somebody about it.

"Mrs. Cottler, do you know anything about sleepwalking?"

The old woman was sitting on the couch, stroking the black cat. She didn't seem to hear Mayra. Finally she looked up. The cat looked up too. "I'm sorry, Mayra. Were you speaking to me?"

"Yes. I—uh—wondered if you knew anything about sleepwalking."

Mrs. Cottler didn't seem at all surprised by the question. "Sleepwalking. Yes. Yes," she said, looking down at Hazel as she answered. "It's very mysterious. Very mysterious." She picked up the cat and began to play with her.

Mayra wiped her hands on the striped dish towel. She decided not to tell Mrs. Cottler what had happened.

"Let's walk later," Mrs. Cottler said, settling back

on the couch. "Let's break our routine and read a few chapters first." Hazel mewed and leapt silently down to the carpet. She curled up in a ball in front of the couch, as if getting comfortable to listen to Mayra read.

After work Mayra wanted to hurry over to Donna's and tell her about the sleepwalking. But she had to go to the mall to get some paint samples for her mother.

She felt relieved to get out of Mrs. Cottler's house, even though the day had gone surprisingly smoothly. Mrs. Cottler was in a very cheerful mood and didn't seem to notice that Mayra was so distracted and lost in her own thoughts. The old woman had dozed off about halfway through the chapter, and Mayra read on quietly, her voice little above a murmur, her mind far away from the words she was reading.

Now the orange afternoon sun was lowering behind the trees. The air smelled fresh and cool. Mayra had to walk past the Fear Street cemetery to get to the bus stop on Park Drive. Two very blond kids, a boy of eight or nine and a girl maybe a few years older, were laughing and chasing each other in a wild game of tag just beyond the cemetery wall.

Why are they playing in there? Mayra wondered. She had a sudden impulse to yell to them, to tell them to go play somewhere else. Hadn't they heard the awful stories about the Fear Street cemetery?

When she was a little girl, a boy from down the block had given her bad dreams for weeks by telling her the story of why the gravestones there were all crooked. It was because the dead people underneath were pushing up with their shoulders, pushing up every night, trying to push the gravestones away so they could climb out. To this day crooked gravestones in a cemetery gave Mayra the shudders.

She started to call out to the two kids, but they were gone. Their high-pitched laughter still rang in her ears. But they were nowhere to be seen. She crossed the street and peered over the wall. Were they hiding from her? There was no sign of them.

As she walked away, she thought she heard them giggling nearby. But it may have been a bird. Or just her imagination.

She crossed the street and stopped.

A man had just stepped out of the house across from the cemetery, closing the door loudly behind him. He's staring at me, Mayra realized. He's looking at me as if he recognizes me!

The man looked very surprised to see her.

He's enormous, Mayra thought, staring back at him. He was nearly seven feet tall, powerfully built, and had a football player's neck, almost wider than his head. He was wearing black spandex bicycle shorts and a red, sleeveless T-shirt that showed off his commanding chest and bulging muscles.

With his square, red-cheeked face and short, blond flat-top haircut, he looked like the stereotype of a marine drill sergeant or a pro football middle line-backer.

What are *you* staring at, Big Neck? Mayra thought.

She looked behind her to make sure he wasn't staring at someone else. No. Fear Street was empty. There was no one else around.

Mayra knew she had never seen him before, but he seemed to recognize her. As he stared, his expression slowly changed from surprise to anger.

Suddenly he started toward her, taking long, quick strides. "Hey!" he shouted, more of a grunt than a word.

He's dangerous, Mayra decided.

She just had a feeling, a sudden cold chill of warning.

He wants to hurt me.

He wants to *get* me.

Maybe it was his size. Maybe it was the intense look on his face. There was something wrong with him.

She turned and started to run.

"Hey—stop!"

Her heart pounding, she ran faster. Was he following her?

She didn't turn around to look.

She didn't stop running until she reached the bus stop. Then, gasping for air, she leaned against the bus-stop pole and looked behind her.

He wasn't there. He hadn't followed.

Very relieved, she clung to the pole, waiting for her heart to stop pounding and her breathing to return to normal.

Who was that man? What did he want?

She was certain she had never seen him before. She surely would have remembered someone so big, so dangerous looking.

The bus came after a few minutes, and she stepped in and paid her fare. She was the only passenger. My own personal air-conditioned limo, she thought. She gratefully slumped into a plastic seat and rested her head against the cool window glass. She felt so tired, so worn out. It wasn't just the run to the bus stop. It was also the sleepwalking the night before. It seemed to have drained all of her energy.

The sleepwalking. Would she do it again tonight?

The Division Street stop came too soon. She wanted to keep riding. It was so cool and calming. She still felt shook up over that weird man. She couldn't get his face out of her mind.

Stepping down, Mayra was surprised by the warm, humid air outside. She crossed the street and headed into the Division Street Mall.

I used to spend so much time here in the summer, she thought. Before I had to have a job . . .

Surprised at how empty the mall was, she stopped to look at some bathing suits at a narrow little store called Clothes Call. She found a green bikini she was tempted to try on. But what was the point? She hadn't brought enough money with her. She had just come for color samples of paint. She couldn't buy the bathing suit even if it looked fabulous on her, which it probably wouldn't.

She walked past the Doughnut Hole. The aroma of cinnamon buns almost pulled her back in, but she managed to resist. Maybe I'll buy a couple to bring home on my way out, she thought.

She suddenly realized she was starving. Stopping in front of Ray's Pizza Place, she peered into the window. A lot of kids from school were there. Maybe one of her friends could be cajoled into sharing a slice or two of pizza.

Wait a minute. Whoa!

Mayra blinked hard. She didn't want to believe her eyes.

Who was that in the center booth?

Yes. It was Walker.

Mayra shielded her eyes and squinted through the window to make sure she wasn't seeing things.

No. She was right. It was Walker. He was sharing a pizza with Suki Thomas, just about the trashiest girl in school.

They were gazing into each other's eyes, and they were holding hands.

chapter
8

Mayra was so startled, she entered the restaurant and walked right up to their booth. "Walker!"

Their hands moved apart. They both smiled up at her.

"Mayra, I didn't see you come in," Walker said, looking at Suki.

"I-I'm having an awful afternoon. A guy chased me!" Mayra blurted out.

"Huh?" they both uttered.

"Some man chased me—on Fear Street—after I got out of Mrs. Cottler's."

Walker's smile faded and his face filled with concern. "What? Who was it? Should we call the police?"

"No. I-I'm sorry. He didn't follow me very far, but—"

"That's frightening," Suki said, shaking her head. Her platinum hair was spiked punk-style with about a ton or two of gel. She wore a purple T-shirt and matching purple tights under jean cutoffs. "What did he look like?"

"He looked dangerous," Mayra said curtly, staring at Walker. "He was really big."

"Mayra, sit down." Walker scooted over to the wall, making room for her.

"No. I don't want to interrupt anything," she said pointedly, giving Walker a dirty look just in case he didn't catch her meaning.

Looking very nervous, Walker immediately started to explain. "I ran into Suki here at the mall. I was going to the magic store to pick up some cards I ordered. And there she was. And we got to talking. Actually, we were talking about *you* when you came in. We were both hungry, so we just got a pizza."

"And you thought you'd stay warm till the pizza arrived by holding hands?"

"Huh?" He looked at her with disbelief. "We weren't."

"Get real, Mayra. We weren't," Suki repeated, shaking her head.

"I was showing her a coin trick. You know, which hand has the coin? That's all."

Those two pink spots on his cheeks. That innocent look on his handsome face. Mayra realized she believed him.

He *had* to be telling the truth. No one could be *that* bad of a liar!

"And where was the coin?" Mayra asked.

Suki shrugged. "I couldn't find it. He's too tricky for me."

Mayra realized she had jumped to the wrong conclusion. Walker was telling the truth. He and Suki had met at the mall and got a pizza. Big deal. She had overreacted. She slid into the booth beside Walker.

What would Walker see in Suki anyway? Never mind. Cancel that question, Mayra thought. Suki had the worst reputation of any girl at Shadyside High. It was easy to figure out what Walker might see in her.

But he wasn't exactly her type. He was so shy and straight. There *couldn't* be anything going on between them. Mayra scolded herself for getting jealous so quickly, for not trusting Walker more.

"What are you doing this summer?" Suki asked Mayra, after slurping the remains of her Coke.

"Working."

"Me too. At least I *was* working," Suki said, sighing. "I was working at Frosty's here at the mall. You know, the hair place. But I got canned. They wanted me to work too many hours. I said, like, forget it, you know. So they said I could forget coming to work."

"Bummer," Mayra said. She realized this was the longest conversation she had ever had with Suki.

"How about some pizza?" Walker asked. He pulled the platter over toward her.

"No. Thanks. I've got to get home. I mean, I've got to do some shopping." Mayra realized she had forgotten all about her mother's color samples. It was nearly dinnertime. She had to hurry.

She climbed out of the booth. "Wait. I'll give you a lift," Walker said.

Mayra really wanted to talk to Walker, to tell him about her sleepwalking episode, how weird and frightening it was. But this definitely was not the time. She already believed him about Suki. She didn't want to hear him explain all over again, which he was sure to do. And she didn't want to have to describe being chased by the big blond man again. He was obviously just some nutcase who mistook her for somebody else or something. She just wanted to forget about him.

"No, thanks. Call me later. Bye, Suki." And she ran out of the restaurant without looking back.

"I hope I don't have to start locking you in at night."

Mayra glared at her mother. "It's not a joke, you know."

Mrs. Barnes took a sip of her coffee and set the mug down on the table. They had just finished dinner and the dishes hadn't been cleared yet. Mayra had waited until they had finished their dinner, a casserole of ground beef and macaroni and cheese, to tell her mother about her sleepwalking. And now her mother was reacting in typical fashion, making a joke of it.

"Why do you always think everything that happens to me is funny?" Mayra demanded.

"I don't, Mayra. Stop looking at me like that. Sleepwalking is serious. But I don't want you to be scared and worried. It will probably never happen again. Please, dear—relax."

"Mother, I nearly walked into the street. What if I hadn't woken up?"

"But you *did* wake up. Look, I'm a nurse. And I can guarantee you that no one has ever come into our hospital because they walked into a truck while walking in their sleep. You're going to be fine."

"Oh, that makes me feel a lot better," Mayra said

sarcastically. She reached across the table and took a sip of her mother's coffee. "Ugh. Don't you put any sweetener in?"

"No. I like it strong. Strong and greasy."

Mayra made a face and shoved the mug back toward her mother.

"You've never walked in your sleep before," Mrs. Barnes said, resting her hand lightly on top of Mayra's. "You don't talk in your sleep as far as I know. You've never even been a restless sleeper."

"True," Mayra agreed.

"So chances are this was one troubling incident. Maybe you were upset about something. Maybe it was something you ate."

"Mother!" Mayra angrily pulled her hand away.

"Okay, okay. It wasn't something you ate. Sorry. I can see that you're very upset. But I think you have to stay calm, keep it in perspective, that's all."

"I was out in the street in my nightgown!"

"If you feel that upset, there's a wonderful man at the hospital you could go talk to."

"You mean a shrink?"

"Yes. He's a friend of mine, and I'm sure he'd make time to see you."

"So you think I'm cracking up?"

"No, of course not. But it might make you feel better to talk to someone. It might be reassuring. Obviously, everything I say, you're just going to jump down my throat."

"I'm not jumping down your throat. But you just think it's funny that I went traipsing around outside in my sleep, and I think it's really scary."

Mrs. Barnes started to say something, but the doorbell rang. She glanced at her watch. "Now, who could that be?"

"Maybe it's Walker," Mayra said, jumping up and jogging quickly toward the front. "I saw him at the mall, and he was worried about me, so . . ."

Mayra ran to the front hallway and pulled open the door. "Stephanie!"

"Hi. How ya doin'?" Stephanie gave her a little wave. She was wearing a navy blue, long-sleeve top with a white scarf around her neck, and white tennis shorts. Her black hair was pulled straight back in a ponytail. Even in the yellow porch light, she looked tan.

She looks so much like Link, Mayra thought.

Mayra opened the screen door and Stephanie walked in. "How'd you get so tan?" Mayra asked. "I heard you were working this summer."

"I am. At Shadyside Day-Care. It's like a day camp. I'm outside with the kids most of the day. So I get a lot of sun."

"Well, hi, Stephanie." Mrs. Barnes came into the hallway. "Don't you look beautiful."

"Thanks, Mrs. Barnes. How are you?"

"Okay. Haven't seen you for quite a while."

Stephanie looked at Mayra, uncomfortable. "Yeah. Well . . . I've been working. At Shadyside Day-Care. I've got twenty four-year-olds in my group. I'm so tired, some nights I go to bed at eight-thirty!"

"Do you sleep indoors or out?" Mrs. Barnes asked, and then laughed.

"Mother, you're not funny!"

Stephanie looked confused. "What's she talking about?"

"Never mind," Mayra said quickly.

Mrs. Barnes retreated back to the kitchen.

"You're not busy or anything?" Stephanie asked. "I should've called first, but—"

"No, no. I'm glad. I mean, I'm happy to see you," Mayra said. She was so relieved that Stephanie wasn't angry at her for breaking up with Link. "Come on up to my room and let's talk."

Stephanie followed her up the stairs. Mayra plopped down in the desk chair and motioned for Stephanie to sit on the bed. "You look very preppy. That scarf looks great with that top. I really like it."

"You *should* like it," Stephanie said, laughing. "It's your scarf."

"It is?"

"Yeah. You left it at our house months ago."

"Oh. Then give it back," Mayra said, only half joking.

"No way. I'm keeping it," Stephanie said, smoothing the scarf with both hands.

Mayra expected her to laugh and hand back the scarf, but she saw that Stephanie was serious. She really intended to keep it.

That's strange, Mayra thought. She probably has a dozen scarves of her own. Stephanie's family was pretty well off, and Stephanie was just about the best-dressed girl at Shadyside High.

There was an uncomfortable silence.

"Hey, I'm putting you on," Stephanie said finally. She removed the scarf from her neck and placed it beside her on the bed. "Here ya go."

Mayra felt strangely relieved. "So you're having a good summer?" she asked.

"Yeah. Kind of. But Link isn't." Stephanie flipped her ponytail back over her shoulder. Her expression changed. All of the friendliness faded from her face.

"Stephanie—" Mayra started, shifting her position on the desk chair, tucking her legs under her. She had a sudden feeling of dread as she realized that Stephanie had a purpose to her visit.

"We have to talk about Link," Stephanie said in a low voice.

"No, we don't," Mayra said quickly. "I know he's your brother, but—"

"You have no right to hurt him like this."

"Yes, I do," Mayra insisted, then immediately wished she hadn't said it. It sounded so cold. "Listen, we can't talk about this. There's nothing to talk about."

"Why did you do it to him, Mayra? You have no idea what you did to him. He's totally wrecked. He counted on you. He cared about you. And then you ruined everything. You—"

"I broke up with him. That's all. It happens, you know. It wasn't working out. I didn't want to hurt him. I had no idea he'd carry on like this. And send his sister to—"

"He didn't send me!" Stephanie shouted.

"Sorry."

"I came on my own just to tell you what a mess Link is. And it's all your fault."

"Sorry," Mayra repeated.

"Sorry isn't enough."

"What else can I say?"

"Say that you'll go back with him. Give it another chance."

"I can't."

"Yes, you can."

"But I don't want to. Listen, Stephanie, Link has to grow up sometime."

"What's that supposed to mean?"

"All this mooning around and following me and calling me—it's so childish. Even if he didn't send you to talk to me, why are you here? Because you think he's childish too. You think he's too childish to deal with his own problems."

"That's not true," Stephanie snapped, her dark eyes flaring. "I came because I care about my brother and because I wanted to tell you what I think of you."

"Well, okay. You've done it. But there's nothing I can say. I'm sorry everyone feels bad. I feel bad too. Really."

"And that's it?" Stephanie jumped to her feet.

"Yeah. 'Fraid so," Mayra said softly.

"You'll be sorry," Stephanie said. At least that's what Mayra thought she said. She hadn't quite heard. "What did you say?"

"I said I'm sorry for you."

"Goodbye, Stephanie," Mayra said wearily. "Have a nice life."

Stephanie flashed her an angry look, turned, and walked quickly from the room. Mayra didn't get up from the desk chair. She listened to Stephanie's heavy footsteps on the stairs, then heard the front door slam shut.

She suddenly realized she was shaking all over. She hated confrontations like that, especially with someone she had considered a friend.

What a shame. It was just such a shame.

She looked over at the bed. The white scarf. It was gone. Stephanie had taken the scarf!

chapter
9

*T*he dream was so vivid.

She could smell the pine air, feel the cold, clear water as she stepped into the lake.

It was a bright, sunny day, so sunny everything seemed to shimmer and gleam. The colors were so intense. She was surrounded by a mist of glowing yellow. Sunshine yellow, so warm, so bright.

Beneath her feet the lake washed blue, cold blue. Gentle ripples caught the sunlight, splashing over her bare ankles.

She walked over the water, walked normally but slowly, her arms at her sides, looking straight ahead, always straight ahead over the widening lake. What a glorious day!

But she could not keep the troublesome thoughts away.

Someone was watching her from the shore. Someone was staring at her as she walked on the lake. Who was it?

She turned back to see. But the glare, the shimmering yellow glare was blinding. She shut her eyes and looked away. The yellow glare formed a curtain. She couldn't see beyond it. She couldn't see who was watching her.

The lake water suddenly felt colder. Low, rippling waves splashed harder against her legs. The yellow sunlight faded to gray, and then black.

Mayra woke up.

Where am I? she thought.

Trees whispered. Wind blew at her nightgown.

I'm outside again in my nightgown, she realized.

Surrounded by trees, tall pines, oaks, low hedges, an overturned tricycle in a gravel driveway, a rambling, old house, dark, one shutter banging against the shingles.

It's not my house, she thought.

I'm not in front of my house. I'm—somewhere else.

Gripped with fear, she realized she'd been holding her breath. She let the air out of her lungs and took a deep breath of cool air.

Where am I?

A single streetlight more than half a block away. Old trees bending and scraping at each other.

She looked down at her feet. So wet, so cold. She was standing in a deep puddle, the soft mud oozing between her toes, up over her ankles.

I'm standing in mud. But where?

She forced herself to breathe again.

The dream returned in all its brightness, and she gasped. How could I walk on the lake? Why was I there?

Why am I here?

She stepped out of the puddle. The wind seemed to die. It was so still, as still as a black-and-white photograph. She seemed to be the only thing that could move.

She walked away from the now-silent trees. Beyond low evergreen bushes she saw a street. Beyond the street a tall, old Victorian house with a pale yellow light, as pale as the moon, in a single upstairs window.

The street looked familiar and unfamiliar at the same time.

Mayra walked toward the streetlight, keeping on the soft shoulder at the edge of the street. She swung her right arm as she walked, slowly at first, then more briskly, holding on to the waist of her cotton nightgown with the other hand.

Was that a street sign just beyond the light?

Yes.

She passed another dark, old house, set far back from the street, its yard a ragged carpet of tall grass and weeds.

Do I know that house? Do I know this street? How far have I walked? Have I walked into another dream?

She hurried up to the street sign.

FEAR STREET.

She looked away, then read it again. It hadn't changed. It still said FEAR STREET.

Why am I here?

She had walked in her sleep to Fear Street, to the edge of the woods. To the edge, she thought. To the edge.

Over the edge. I've gone over the edge.

The phrase repeated itself in her mind until it lost all meaning. She looked up at the street sign again. It was real. It was no dream. She was on Fear Street in her nightgown in the middle of the night. She had sleepwalked here . . . to find—what?

She might have stood there forever, staring up at the black-and-white street sign. But the flashing red lights broke into her consciousness, and she realized she was no longer alone.

A car door slammed.

A man walked toward her. The red light flashed. It seemed to surround her. She tried to blink it away.

She knew it was just the dream, coming back once again to frighten her. She looked down, expecting to see the cool, blue lake water. But she saw only dirt.

"Miss?"

The man was right in front of her, standing in the flashing red glow.

"Miss? What are you doing out here?"

He was a policeman. Behind him she saw the flashing red light on the roof of his police car.

"Hi. I—I don't know," Mayra stammered.

"Are you okay?"

"Yes, I think so."

"Have you been hurt? Did someone bring you here?"

"No."

He took her arm gently. She followed him toward the flashing red light. "Can I take you home? Do you live around here?"

"Thank you, Officer."

* * *

Mayra's mother took it very seriously this time.

She came running to the front door, wearing the striped men's pajamas she always wore, and her face filled with fear and surprise when she saw Mayra and the grim-faced policeman.

She led Mayra into the kitchen, her arm tightly around Mayra's waist. Both of them blinked against the harsh kitchen light. Mrs. Barnes put on the kettle to make hot chocolate.

Mayra told her mother about the dream and about waking up on Fear Street. "I can't remember anything else. I can't explain anything else," Mayra said, about to burst into tears.

Mrs. Barnes came up behind her and gave her a hug. "Ssshhh. You're okay now."

"But what is happening to me? Why am I doing this?"

"I don't know," her mother said, pouring the packet of brown chocolate powder into a mug. "I don't know anything about sleepwalking. But the main thing is not to worry, not to get overly upset."

"Overly upset?" Mayra shrieked. She knew her mother was speaking so softly, so calmly in order to calm her down, but it was only making her angry. "How can I not be overly upset? I walked all the way to Fear Street in my sleep!"

"I know, darling," her mother said. She poured the steaming water into the mug and slid it across the counter to Mayra.

"Mom, I can't—"

"Dr. Sterne is on vacation this week," Mrs. Barnes interrupted. "But as soon as he's back in the hospital, we'll go see him."

"What can he say?" Mayra asked miserably. She took a sip of the hot chocolate and burned her tongue.

"Well, I don't know. I think he can probably explain what sleepwalking is. I mean, what causes it."

"Craziness. That's what causes it," Mayra muttered, spreading both hands around the warm mug. "I'm cracking up."

"Stop it. Stop saying that." Mrs. Barnes suddenly looked very tired. "You're not cracking up. There's just something going on that we don't understand. Dr. Sterne is a wonderful man. He'll help us. In the meantime, do you want to sleep with me in my room? Come on. We'll have a sleep-over."

"Thanks, Mom. But, really, I'm fine now. This hot chocolate is doing the trick. I'm feeling a lot calmer, Nurse Nancy." Mayra gave her mother a smile, then took another sip from the mug.

"Maybe we can move Kim into your room for a while," her mother suggested. "She's such a light sleeper, she'd be bound to hear you when you got up. Then she could—"

They were both startled by loud footsteps. Kim came marching into the room in her Garfield the Cat pajamas, her eyes closed, her arms stretched straight out in front of her. "I'm a sleepwalker," she moaned in her impression of a ghostly voice. "I'm a sleepwalker . . ."

"Kim!" Mayra screamed, not at all amused by her sister's performance.

"Have you been listening to us the whole while?" Mrs. Barnes demanded.

Kim ignored them both and continued walking

across the kitchen zombielike, her eyes closed. "I'm a sleepwalker. Watch out for the sleepwalker."

"Stop it, Kim. It isn't funny," Mrs. Barnes said.

"She's just impossible," Mayra said, shaking her head.

Kim finally opened her eyes. "I can sleepwalk too, you know."

"What are you doing up? You have to get up early for camp, remember?" Mrs. Barnes said, putting her hands on Kim's small shoulders, turning her around, and guiding her out of the kitchen.

"I'm not up. I'm sleepwalking," Kim insisted.

A few minutes later Mayra was back in bed. She felt tired, worn out, even. But she couldn't fall asleep.

Every time she'd start to drift off, she forced herself back to alertness.

No, I can't, she thought. I can't let myself have the dream again.

She stared up at the ceiling, feeling more and more frightened.

I may never go to sleep again, she thought.

chapter

10

Walker was so worried about Mayra, he came running over to her house before she left for work. He looked really good in faded jean cutoffs and a red- and white- striped polo shirt.

Mayra was glad to see him, but she said, "You didn't have to rush over here this morning. I'm fine. Really."

"I wanted to," he told her, sitting down awkwardly on the living-room rug, stretching his long legs in front of him. "Come sit down."

"I can't. I'm already late to Mrs. Cottler's."

"A few more minutes won't hurt." He reached up and pulled her down beside him.

"Don't be evil," she said with a grin. She kissed him on the cheek. She liked it when he was forceful, insistent. It happened so rarely.

"Tell me about last night."

"I already told you on the phone. There isn't anything else to say."

"Weird," he said.

"Weird? That's it? That's your opinion?"

"Yeah." He suddenly became thoughtful. "Yeah, it's weird."

"Oh. I thought you meant *I'm* weird."

"Well, that too."

"Thanks a heap. Can't you be serious? I'm really scared."

"I'm serious. I'm scared too. For you, I mean. It must be so weird to wake up someplace outside."

"Not just outside. On Fear Street."

"You know, I have an idea." He scooted back against the couch. "Maybe I could hypnotize you and try to find out what your problem is, or what the dream means, or something."

"No, thanks," Mayra said quickly. She started to get up, but he pulled her back down.

"No. I'm serious. I've been practicing. I mean, I think I'm getting better at it. It's worth a try, don't you think?"

"Walker, *you're* weird," Mayra said, getting up and walking to the mirror in the hallway. She could see his reflection in the mirror as she straightened her T-shirt. He looked genuinely hurt. "I meant that as a compliment," she told him. But his unhappy expression didn't change.

"So you're going to see this shrink?"

"Yeah. As soon as he gets back from vacation. Mom says he's a real nice guy. He's done some kind of sleep research, so maybe he'll know how to stop me from sleepwalking."

Walker climbed to his feet and came up behind her. She looked at him in the mirror. He's so good-looking, she thought. I'd better get to work. She suddenly wasn't sure she could trust herself all alone in the house with him. She had the feeling that if he put his arms around her now, or kissed her, she'd never get to Mrs. Cottler's.

But he didn't.

He looked at her reflection in the mirror for the longest time. Then he asked, "Can I walk you to work?"

"Yeah. Thanks." She wondered if he could see how disappointed she was.

The black cat stared up at Mayra, tilting her head, the yellow green eyes seeming to grow larger. "Hazel," Mayra said, "where is Mrs. Cottler?"

The old woman hadn't answered the door. Mayra had let herself in after knocking several times. She had been greeted by the cat, a wary greeting, as if Hazel were suspicious of Mayra's intentions.

"Mrs. Cottler? Mrs. Cottler?"

No response.

"Maybe she's upstairs," Mayra said aloud.

The cat headed to the stairs as if she understood what Mayra had said.

"Mrs. Cottler?" Mayra called. There was no response, so she climbed the stairs.

The door to Mrs. Cottler's bedroom was open. Mayra peeked inside. The room was empty. But Mayra could see that the bathroom door against the far wall was closed. Mayra stepped into the room. "Mrs. Cottler?"

She could hear the shower going in the bathroom.

So that's where Mrs. Cottler was. Mayra turned to leave when something on the dresser caught her eye. She walked over to it. It was a black candle in a black candle holder. The candle had been burned down to a stub, a puddle of melted black wax surrounded it.

Next to the candle was a small jewelry box, open. Inside it Mayra could see her pale blue beads piled on top of each other. Mrs. Cottler hadn't even begun to string them yet. Why were they out? Why were they here next to this strange-looking black candle?

The water in the shower abruptly stopped.

I'd better get out of here before she sees me, Mayra thought. She turned and hurried silently from the bedroom.

Mayra was preparing lunch, a tuna-fish salad, when Mrs. Cottler finally appeared in the kitchen, leaning on her cane, a guilty smile on her face.

"I'm afraid I overslept this morning," she told Mayra. "It's one of the few pleasures left to an old lady."

"It's a very pretty day," Mayra said, thinking about her beads in the little jewelry box. "Lunch is almost ready."

Mrs. Cottler stepped up to the counter beside Mayra. "You look tired, Mayra," she said, a look of concern wrinkling her normally smooth face.

"Yeah. I know. I haven't been sleeping too well."

"Maybe your mother should make you go to bed a little earlier," Mrs. Cottler said, a strange smile on her face. "By the way, dear, how is your mother?"

So she *does* remember my mother, after all, Mayra realized.

A thunderstorm prevented them from taking their walk down by the lake. "It's just as well," Mrs. Cottler said wistfully. "I only think of Vincent when I go down there. I guess it's my way of remembering him, of keeping him in my life. But it always saddens me."

"We'll read some extra chapters today," Mayra said, smiling warmly, trying to cheer the old woman up. Her dream flashed into her mind suddenly. She saw the lake, the lake of the dream, sparkling and clear. Forcing the image out of her mind, she picked up the book and searched for the chapter.

A few hours later it was still drizzling as Mayra left work. The cold rain felt good on her face. Walking quickly, she headed down Fear Street, eager to get home.

She was halfway past the Fear Street cemetery, her sneakers splashing on the puddle-strewn street, when she heard footsteps behind her.

Was it the man who had followed her before, the man with the big neck?

She shuddered and began walking faster.

Who was he? What did he want?

"Hey—Mayra!"

She spun around.

It wasn't that frightening man. It was Link.

"Link? What are you doing here on Fear Street?"

He smoothed back his dark hair, which was wet from rainwater, and grinned at her. "Waiting for you." He was wearing black denim jeans and a shiny, sleeveless blue T-shirt. His arms and chest were very tanned.

She didn't return his smile. "Link, don't start. I don't want—"

"No. Just kidding," he said, hurrying to catch up to her. "I had a delivery to make. Then I saw you come out, so—"

She looked behind him to the red pickup truck in the middle of the street. Link had left the door on the driver's side wide open. "Is that your truck?"

"Well, they let me drive it for deliveries," he said, grinning again. "Want to go for a ride?" He reached for her hand, but she pulled it away from him.

"No. I don't think so." She suddenly thought of Walker. She wondered what he was doing right this moment. She decided to call him as soon as she got home.

"I'll give you a lift home. Come on, Mayra. It looks like it's going to start pouring again."

"No," she insisted.

"I'll just drive you home. I won't say a word. Promise."

Mayra hesitated, looking up at the darkening sky. "You promise you won't ask me out or anything, Link?"

He raised his right hand as if swearing to it. "No. Nothing as horrible as that," he said, and laughed.

She followed him to the truck and pulled open the passenger door. "Just use that step to climb up," he told her.

Mayra slumped onto the seat and closed the door. She watched Link jog around the front of the truck and hop up to open the door on the driver's side. He looks great, she thought.

Link slid behind the wheel and flashed her a devilish smile. "You look tired. I know just what you need. A long, relaxing ride will cool you out," he said, putting a warm hand on her shoulder. "Why don't we drive up by the River Road?"

Mayra playfully slapped his hand away. "Link— you promised!" She reached for the door handle, but made it clear she was only teasing.

He started up the truck and headed down Fear Street. "Know who I saw yesterday? Kerry Post."

"Oh, yeah?" Kerry was a good friend of Link's who went to South, the other high school in town. She liked Kerry and realized she hadn't thought about him since she'd broken up with Link. "How is he?"

"Weird as ever." Link turned right onto Park Drive. "Know what he's doing this summer? He's a Mister Frostycone Man."

"You're kidding!" Mayra laughed. "You mean he has to dress up like a big ice-cream cone like all those guys?"

"Yep. He has a route for his ice-cream wagon. In the Old Village, I think. Has to ring a bell all day long. I told him I always knew he was a Cone Head!"

Mayra laughed. "And where's his nutty girlfriend Alice?"

"She's spending the summer avoiding Kerry, I think!"

They both laughed. She looked at Link, studied his handsome face. She had forgotten how much fun he could be. It was nice to be with him, so comfortable, so much like old times.

He saw her studying him. He put his hand back on her shoulder. "How about that drive to the River Road?" he said softly. "Just to talk."

She started to say yes. After all, what was the harm?

He squeezed her shoulder.

No, she thought. This is wrong.

Walker's face flashed into her mind.

It's over between Link and me. Sure, he's a great guy. Sure, I miss him sometimes, and the friends we had together. Sure, I can feel comfortable with him. But I'm going with Walker now.

"Link, just take me home," she said, staring straight out the windshield.

She turned in time to see the disappointed look on his face. Link was more than disappointed, she realized. He was furious, seething with anger at being rejected once again.

They rode the rest of the way to her house in silence, grim, tense silence.

He let her off at the curb, and Mayra ran up the driveway without saying goodbye. To her surprise, she found Donna waiting on the front porch. She was wearing Day-Glo-green short-shorts and a matching midriff top. The outfit made her look even tinier than she was.

"Who was that who dropped you off?" Donna asked, giving Mayra a funny look.

"Link," Mayra answered quickly. "Now change the subject."

Donna shrugged. "He doesn't give up, huh?"

"I don't call that changing the subject," Mayra

replied sharply, finding her key and opening the front door.

Donna followed her into the living room, which was cool and pleasant. "Okay. New subject. How's Mrs. Cottler?" Donna asked, flopping down on the big leather couch against the wall.

"Weird," Mayra told her.

"Should I change the subject again?" Donna asked, stretching her legs out, resting her feet on the glass coffee table. "I ran into Walker at the mall. He told me you—uh—went sleepwalking again."

"I was going to call you," Mayra said.

"Want to talk about it?"

Mayra sighed. "There's not much to say."

"You're real talkative today," Donna muttered.

Mayra was still thinking about Link, about how she had been so drawn to him in the truck. It took the two friends a while to get a conversation going, as if they were strangers who didn't know each other at all. At first they talked about small, unimportant matters, as if easing into the conversation. Donna's cousin's new haircut. The cute, little red Porsche that Pete Goodwin's parents had bought. The new Tom Cruise movie.

"Oh, by the way, there was a man here looking for you," Donna said suddenly.

"Huh?"

"Said his name was Cal something-or-other. Do you know him?"

"No," Mayra said, a feeling of dread starting to build in her stomach. "What did he want?"

"I don't know. He came walking up to the porch

while I was waiting for you. A big guy, really big with huge muscles and a neck out to here."

"Oh, no."

"Mayra—are you okay? You look so pale."

"Yeah. I'm okay. I guess. How did he find out where I live? Did he say?"

"No. Uh—oh, yeah. He said Mrs. Cottler gave him the address."

Mrs. Cottler? This Cal knew Mrs. Cottler? Why did she tell him Mayra's address?

"What did he want?"

"He didn't say. I told him you weren't home. I hope I did the right thing," Donna said. "He was kinda creepy."

"Yeah, he is," Mayra said. She told Donna about her first encounter with Cal outside the Fear Street cemetery.

"Oh, well. Maybe he just wants to sell you a magazine subscription," Donna said, leaning back against the couch and staring up at the shadows playing across the white ceiling.

"Yeah. For sure," Mayra said sarcastically.

"So why are you sleepwalking?" Donna asked abruptly.

It took Mayra a few seconds to change gears. "Wish I knew," she replied after a bit.

"I saw a movie where this woman sleepwalked every night," Donna said, scratching her knee.

"Oh, nice," Mayra groaned. "I guess you're going to tell me about it, right?"

"Right. She sleepwalked because she wanted to kill this guy."

"Donna—please—"

"Only she was too afraid to kill him while she was awake. So she sleepwalked and killed him in her sleep. Then they couldn't try her for murder because she was asleep when she did it."

"Donna—give me a break!" Mayra pleaded.

"Maybe you'd like to kill somebody," Donna suggested.

"Yes. You!" Mayra said, walking over to where Donna was sitting. She wrapped her fingers around Donna's neck and did a little playful choking.

"Okay, okay. What's your theory?" Donna asked.

"My theory?"

"About your sleepwalking."

"My theory is—" Mayra started. And then the idea came to her all at once, like a sudden explosion that clears everything out of its path, and she felt shaken by the certainty of it even as she thought about it. "My theory is that Mrs. Cottler is a witch and that she is casting a spell on me to make me sleepwalk."

Donna laughed. "Good one, Mayra. That's as good as my movie plot!"

Mayra laughed too.

But she pictured the old woman sitting so straight on her bed with her eyes closed. And she thought of the burnt black candle and of her beads on the dresser and of Stephanie saying that a witch needs a possession of yours to cast a spell on you—and she knew in her heart of hearts that her theory was right.

chapter

11

"Mom, can I quit my job with Mrs. Cottler?"

Mrs. Barnes, wearing a red- and white-striped apron over her chinos and T-shirt, flipped the hamburgers one by one on the charcoal grill, squinting against the smoke.

"Mom, did you hear me?" Mayra asked, coming closer.

"No. Sorry. Did you say something, dear? These hamburgers are almost done. Call Kim and Donna."

"But I asked you a question," Mayra insisted, not meaning to sound so whiny. "Is it okay if I quit my job?"

Mrs. Barnes frowned. She slapped a mosquito off her arm with the barbecue mitt. "I thought we weren't going to talk about anything serious. That's why we came up here to Lake Monolac, remember? To get you away for the weekend, away from everything that's been troubling you."

It was one of her mom's spur-of-the-moment ideas, and it had seemed like a good one to Mayra at the time. Her Uncle George had a spacious, three-bedroom cabin on the lake that they could use. And Mrs. Barnes said she could bring Donna along for company.

A change of scenery seemed to be just what the doctor ordered. A weekend by the most beautiful lake in the state, far away from Mrs. Cottler, far away from Fear Street, from everything—Mayra had quickly agreed.

She had to break a date with Walker. He sounded disappointed, but he was very understanding. "Get going," he said. "Have fun. And don't think about anything heavy."

But it wasn't as easy as she had thought to run away from her thoughts. Saturday afternoon, she and Donna had rowed out to the middle of the lake in her uncle's rowboat. Donna was wearing the same Day-Glo short-shorts and midriff top she had on the Tuesday afternoon. Mayra was wearing a long green T-shirt over a white one-piece bathing suit. It was a beautiful day, and the lake sparkled under the sunlight like a fairy-tale version of a lake.

"Isn't this fantastic?" Donna asked.

"What?" Mayra was lost in her own thoughts. She had been thinking of Mrs. Cottler, of her beads, of sleepwalking to Fear Street, where Mrs. Cottler lived.

It was all so obvious now. Mrs. Cottler was crazy! She was using Mayra to get revenge on Mayra's mother. She hadn't forgotten the hospital stay, the supposed poor care she had received from Mrs. Barnes. She was casting the sleepwalking spell on Mayra to pay Mayra's mother back.

I have to do two things, she told herself. I have to get my beads back. And I have to quit my job, to get as far away from Mrs. Cottler as possible.

She suddenly realized that Donna was standing up in the rowboat. "Donna—what are you doing?"

Donna laughed. "Just trying to get your attention. I've been talking to you for the last five minutes. I don't think you heard a word I said."

"Sorry. I was just—I don't know—thinking."

"That's a bad habit," Donna said, sitting down cross-legged. The boat bobbed gently on the blue green water. Donna tried to carry on a conversation, talking about what she planned to do after her senior year at Shadyside High, but Mayra just couldn't concentrate. After a while Donna gave up trying, and the two girls lay back in silence in the small boat, staring up at the puffy clouds that drifted overhead.

Mayra spent the rest of the afternoon alone in the cabin, trying to rest. When she emerged that evening, Donna was playing with Kim along the pebbly shore. Her mother was tending the smoky barbecue. "So can I quit my job?" Mayra asked.

"We really do need the money," Mrs. Barnes said, concentrating on the blackening hamburgers. "It's such an easy job, Mayra. Why do you want to quit?"

Why?

What could Mayra say? She couldn't tell her mother the real reason she wanted to quit: "Mrs. Cottler is a witch. She's casting a sleepwalking spell on me." Oh, that would really go over big. Her mother would laugh for weeks over that one.

"Uh—I just want to quit." Pretty lame.

"Stick with the job," Mrs. Barnes said, closing her eyes as the wind shifted the smoke toward her face. "It's not like you to be a quitter. Just think of all the new clothes you'll be able to buy before school in the fall."

"But, Mom—I think the job has something to do with my sleepwalking," Mayra said. She hadn't intended to say it, and regretted it immediately.

Mrs. Barnes gave her an exasperated frown. "If you're going to start sleepwalking every time you take a job, you're going to have a very hard time in life, Mayra."

"That—that's not what I meant," Mayra stammered. "Oh, never mind." She turned and began walking quickly away to call Donna and Kim for dinner. She felt very foolish.

Kim and Donna were on the narrow, sandy ledge of beach along the shore. They had been joined by a friend Kim had made, a boy named Andy, two or three years younger than Kim. They were busily digging a deep hole in the sand.

As Mayra approached, Kim jumped up and dropped her sand shovel. "Watch this," she said to Donna and Andy. "Guess who I am."

She closed her eyes, stretched her arms straight out in front of her, and began walking stiff-legged across the sand, snoring loudly.

"I get it. You're Mayra!" Donna cried, trying unsuccessfully to stifle her laughter.

"That's not funny. Don't encourage her," Mayra snapped angrily.

Donna shrugged. Kim lowered her arms and opened her eyes. "It is *so* funny, stupid."

"Kim, don't call me stupid. Listen, I'm afraid it's time for Andy to go find his parents. It's dinnertime."

"Watch this," Andy said, grinning at Mayra. He had a red plastic car in his hand. Suddenly he pulled his arm back and heaved the car into the water.

Mayra watched as the car hit with a splash and then coasted over the gentle, lapping current.

"It floats," Andy said with some pride.

"NO!" Mayra shrieked, startling everyone. Staring at the little red car in the water, she held both hands over her ears as if trying to shut out the world.

"NO! NO! NO! NO!" she cried.

Mrs. Barnes dropped her spatula and came running down to the beach. "What's the matter, Mayra?"

"NO! NO! NO! NO! NO!"

It took several minutes to calm her down.

Even then, Mayra couldn't explain why she had screamed.

chapter
12

"*D*onna, you're late."

Donna shrugged. "Sorry. I had to do some chores for my mom." She was wearing a faded Hard Rock Cafe T-shirt and jean cutoffs. "It's really nice of your mom to let me borrow the car."

"Well, she carpools to the hospital some mornings." Mayra glanced nervously at her watch, then handed Donna the car keys. "She said the tank is full."

"It's such a drag having an orthodontist all the way over in Waynesbridge," Donna said. "There's no bus that lets me off anywhere near his office. Thanks again." She started out the door, then abruptly turned back. "How are you feeling?"

"Me? Fine," Mayra answered quickly.

"Good. You look kind of nervous or something."

"No. It's just that I'm late for work."

"Sorry again," Donna said. "You can tell Mrs. Cottler it was my fault."

"Then she'd probably cast a spell on you too," Mayra said. She meant it to be funny, but it came out very serious.

"Are you sure you're okay?" Donna held the screen door open, half in, half out of the house.

"Yeah. I guess. I don't know what happened to me up at the lake. I—I was just overtired, I guess."

"You haven't been sleeping?"

"I'm afraid to sleep," Mayra confided. "I'm afraid that if I fall asleep, I'll have the dream again. And if I have the dream again, I'll sleepwalk again. So I—"

"You force yourself to stay awake?"

"Yeah."

"That's weird," Donna said, shaking her head sympathetically.

"Yeah. It's weird all right," Mayra said with some bitterness. She looked at her watch again and playfully but forcefully pushed Donna out the door. "Go. Go. Go. Go to your orthodontist. Now I'm really late."

"Okay, okay. I'm going. You know, Mayra, maybe you should quit this job."

"My mom won't let me." Mayra pulled the front door closed behind her and followed her friend down the walk. "How about giving me a lift? It's starting to rain."

"Sorry. No room," Donna cracked. Mayra didn't smile. "Hey—it was a joke."

"Pretty lame," Mayra said sullenly, yawning.

"You're no fun when you don't sleep," Donna said, pulling open the door to the Toyota and sliding behind the wheel.

"It's not a fun summer," Mayra said wistfully,

glancing at her watch, thinking about the old woman waiting for her in that creepy house by the lake.

As she climbed out of the car and said goodbye to Donna, Mayra saw Mrs. Cottler watching her from the front door. "Good morning, Mrs. Cottler," she called. But the old woman seemed to be staring at Donna and didn't respond.

Mayra hurried up to the front stoop. Mrs. Cottler was dressed all in white, a long-sleeved, white blouse over a pleated white skirt. With her jet black hair and rosy complexion she looked about half her age.

"Mayra, I need to talk to you," she said, leaning on her cane with one hand, pushing open the screen door with the other.

"I-I'm really sorry I'm late, Mrs. Cottler," Mayra stammered, stepping into the house, which was cool despite the heat of the day. "I had to wait for my friend and—"

"That's okay," Mrs. Cottler said quickly. She turned and slowly walked past the cluttered living room to the kitchen. "I have something to tell you."

Is she going to confess about casting a spell on me? That was Mayra's first thought.

Is she going to fire me? Her second thought.

A feeling of dread formed in the pit of her stomach. She suddenly felt very cold. Why was it so chilly in this house? The temperature was at least eighty-five outside.

Mrs. Cottler leaned against the kitchen counter and smiled. "I'm going to be going away for a few days."

"Oh!" The word just slipped out of Mayra's mouth,

a quiet cry of surprise. That wasn't what she had been expecting Mrs. Cottler to say at all.

"My sister isn't well. I'm going up to Vermont to check on her," Mrs. Cottler continued, fussing with the front of her white blouse.

"So you won't be needing me?" Mayra asked, trying not to sound happy about it. But inside she was jumping up and down for joy.

"Well, I can't take Hazel with me. So I'd like you to come feed her every day. And while you're here, you can take in the mail and water the plants."

"Sure. That's fine!" Mayra exclaimed. She'll be gone, she told herself. Gone. Gone. Maybe for those few days I'll be able to sleep peacefully again.

"Of course, I'll pay your full salary," Mrs. Cottler said, heading to the sink.

"Oh. Thanks." I'll pay *you* to go away, Mayra thought. "That's very generous of you, Mrs. Cottler."

"Well, I know you'll take good care of Hazel and the house while I'm away." Hazel stared up doubtfully at Mayra. The cat was staying close by Mrs. Cottler's ankles this morning, as if she knew her owner would soon be leaving her.

"Yes. I'll come every day without fail," Mayra said. "When are you leaving?" She hoped she didn't sound too eager.

"Tomorrow morning. My sister's husband is driving down today to pick me up." Leaning on her cane, Mrs. Cottler moved to the sink. "Gracious. I forgot I was in the middle of something here."

She picked up a heavy meat cleaver, the kind Mayra had only seen at the butcher shop, and began chopping away at something, raising the cleaver high and bringing it down hard with a loud crash.

Mayra moved closer to the sink to see what the old woman was cutting with such ferocity. Then she sank back, groaning, feeling sick.

It looked like a human hand.

Mrs. Cottler, a strange smile on her face, turned and caught Mayra's expression. "Mayra—what's the matter?" she asked, holding the cleaver high, about to bring it down again.

"That thing you're chopping—" Mayra pointed.

Mrs. Cottler laughed. "What's the matter? Haven't you ever seen pigs' knuckles before? My sister loves pigs' knuckles." She turned back to her work.

Pigs' knuckles? They didn't look like that—did they?

Chop, chop, chop.

Mrs. Cottler had such a gleeful expression on her face as she raised the cleaver and brought it down.

Chop. Chop. Chop. . . .

Feeling tired and unsettled after work, Mayra walked home in the warm rain. She fumbled with the keys, then let herself into the house.

"Mom—are you home?" she called.

No reply.

She walked into the kitchen and looked up at the brass clock over the sink. Four-thirty. Kim would be home from day camp in half an hour.

As she opened the refrigerator to look for a cold drink, the phone rang. She picked it up after the first ring.

"Hi, Mayra." It was her mother. "I'm still at the hospital. There's been an accident."

Mayra suddenly felt cold all over. "An accident?"

"Yes. Donna. She's here. In the hospital. In my ward. I—uh—well— She's been in a bad accident with the car."

chapter

13

"*D*onna, you sound weird." Mayra was gripping the receiver so tightly, her hand began to hurt.

"Yeah. I know." Donna's voice sounded hoarse and far away. She spoke slowly, as if just waking up from a long sleep. "I guess it's the painkillers they gave me."

"Are you in a lot of pain?"

There was a long silence. "No. Not anymore. I—just a minute, Mayra. A nurse just came in to give me more medicine."

Mayra paced back and forth across the kitchen floor. Thank God she's alive, she thought. She's going to be okay.

"I'm back," Donna said, her voice just a whisper now. "I'm okay, I think, Mayra."

"My mom said you have a broken leg."

"Yeah. And a broken wrist. And some bruised ribs."

For some reason Mayra pictured Mrs. Cottler with

her cleaver, chopping, chopping away at the pigs' knuckles.

"Your mom's been really great," Donna said. "I kind of freaked when I saw the tube in my arm. But she was cool. She explained everything. I'm lucky, I guess."

"Lucky?" Mayra's hands were sweaty. She tucked the phone under her chin and continued to pace.

"Well, that nut was trying to kill me. I'm sure of it."

For a moment Mayra couldn't say anything. That nut? What was Donna talking about?

The painkillers the nurses were giving her must be making her a little strange, Mayra thought. "Donna, what did you just say?"

"I said he tried to run me off the highway. I mean, he *did* run me off the highway."

"Who?"

"I don't know. I only saw his truck. It was raining so hard. And he had his sun visor down in front of the windshield so I couldn't see his face."

"Truck? Someone in a truck tried to run you down?"

"Yeah. He came up from behind and started bumping me. I was scared out of my mind. I sped up. Tried to get away. But he started bumping me harder, harder. It was so slippery because of the rain. I was on the highway, and there was no place to turn off. No place . . ."

Donna seemed to drift away. "Donna—are you still there? Are you okay?"

"Then he just plowed into me from the side. He must have been going really fast. And of course the truck was bigger—so much bigger than the little Toyota. I—I guess I lost control."

"And you crashed?"

"There was a barrier by the side of the highway. A concrete barrier. I crashed into it. I hit hard and bounced a few times. Glass was shattering. It seemed to be shattering all around me. I don't think I'll ever forget that sound. It was like the whole world was cracking. Falling to bits. Oh, I'm so tired, Mayra. My eyelids feel like weights."

Mayra had a horrible thought. "Donna—what color was the truck?"

"It was a pickup truck."

"Yes, but what color was it?"

"Huh?"

"Think hard. You must remember."

"It was . . . uh . . . red. A red pickup truck. I've got to sleep now, Mayra." Her voice was just a whisper. "These pills . . ."

"Bye, Donna. I'll come visit you." She waited for a reply, but Donna must have drifted off to sleep.

Link's pickup truck was red, she thought.

And Link was so furious at me when I rejected him, so furious he couldn't speak.

She replaced the phone receiver and realized she was shivering. Her whole body was shivering. Not cold shivers. Shivers that started in her brain and worked their way down. Shivers of the mind. Shivers of fright.

It couldn't have been Link, she thought, wrapping her arms around herself, trying to stop the shuddering. It couldn't have been Link.

But whoever it was, he wasn't trying to get Donna.

Donna was driving *my* car.

He was trying to get me.

Walker hung up the phone quickly as Mayra entered his room. "Oh, hi. I wasn't expecting you." He looked more than a little flustered. The two spots on his cheeks were bright scarlet. He was wearing white tennis shorts and a white, sleeveless T-shirt.

"Talking to your girlfriend?" Mayra teased.

"Ha, ha. Very funny."

She kissed him on the cheek. "Hi, stranger."

"What are you doing here?" he asked. Mayra had imagined a warmer greeting.

"I wanted to talk to you. I have a lot to tell you about."

He walked past her to the window. The sun had just gone down behind the trees, but the air was still hot and sticky. He stared out into the gray.

"Your mom said it was okay to come up," Mayra said, suddenly feeling like an intruder.

"That's okay," Walker said, without turning around.

"Well, aren't you glad to see me?" she asked. Why did she have to plead with him to be friendly? Was it just his shyness?

"Of course I am." He walked over and put his arm around her shoulders. "I want to show you a new trick."

"No. Come on, Walker. No tricks tonight. I want to talk to you. I really *need* to talk."

He looked disappointed. "Well, okay. Come on downstairs. We'll sit in the den. You can tell me everything."

That's more like it, Mayra thought. She followed him downstairs to the den. They sat close together on the leather couch and talked without interruption for nearly two hours.

She told him about Donna and the red pickup truck. She told him about Cal, the man who had been following her and asking about her. And she told him her theory that Mrs. Cottler had cast a spell on her to make her sleepwalk.

"You're going to laugh at me. I know it," she had said before launching into her theory.

But Walker hadn't laughed. His face grew serious as she talked, and he began to nod in agreement.

"You may be right," he said when she had finished.

"You don't think I'm going wacko?"

"No. Witches aren't only in storybooks," Walker said seriously. They were sitting side by side, pressing against each other despite the heat of the room. He had his long legs crossed and one arm draped behind her on the back of the couch.

She wanted to kiss him, but he was so tall, his face was out of reach. Besides, she decided not to distract him now. She wanted to hear what he had to say.

"I've read a lot about witches and their covens," he said. "There are more witches today than there were in historical times. They keep pretty quiet about it, but they're here."

"And is it possible for a witch to cast a sleepwalking spell on someone?" she asked, leaning against him.

"There are all kinds of spells," he said thoughtfully. "My question is, why? What's the reason someone might want to do that to you?"

"Well, I'm not really sure. But Mrs. Cottler was in the hospital a while back, and my mother was her nurse. And somehow Mrs. Cottler got the crazy idea that my mother was trying to kill her. She complained to the hospital and made a big fuss."

"And you think—"

"That she hired me and cast a spell on me to pay back my mother."

"Weird," he said, shaking his head.

"Oh, I forgot to tell you, Mrs. Cottler is going away for a couple of days."

"Perfect!" Walker cried, jumping up from the couch.

"Huh? What do you mean? I still have to go over there to feed her cat. I can't spend all day playing with you."

"Even more perfect," he said. "That gives us a couple of days to investigate. We'll go over there together tomorrow, and we'll search her house. We'll find out if she's a witch. And if she is, we'll look for clues."

Mayra squeezed Walker's hand. "Great! You'll come with me? Really?"

"Of course," he said. "I don't like to see you like this, so nervous all the time. So tired. We have to find out who is doing this to you. We just have to."

"Thank you," she said gratefully. "And thank you for believing me."

She rushed into his arms and they kissed long and passionately, until his mother walked in to ask if they'd like a snack.

* * *

"Why, Hazel, you've never acted so glad to see me."
The cat rubbed against Mayra's ankles, meowing
loudly. "I'll bet you're hungry. Is that it?"

Mayra turned back to Walker, holding open the
screen door for him. "Come on inside. Don't let the
cat out."

Walker stepped in quickly, staring down at the cat.
"A black cat. Well, that *proves* the old lady is a witch!"

"Hey—I thought you were going to be serious
about this," Mayra scolded.

"I'm serious," Walker said, stepping past her into
Mrs. Cottler's living room. The room was nearly as
dark as night. The heavy curtains were drawn, keeping
out the bright morning sunlight. He walked over and
pulled open the curtains. The sunlight poured over
the cluttered room. "Wow! Look at all this junk!"

"Mrs. Cottler is a real collector," Mayra said,
bending down to pet the cat. "Look around while I
feed Hazel."

She started to the kitchen, but the cat didn't follow.
Instead, she stared suspiciously at Walker. "Come on,
Hazel. Don't you want to eat? Don't pay any attention
to Walker. He won't hurt anything. He's just looking
around."

The cat meowed loudly as if warning Walker, and
then reluctantly followed Mayra into the kitchen. She
began hungrily lapping up the cat food as soon as
Mayra lowered her dish to the floor, and Mayra
hurried to rejoin Walker in the living room.

The house felt even stranger without Mrs. Cottler in
it. The ceiling creaked as if someone were walking
around upstairs. The air seemed thick and musty. The

house smelled of mildew and decay, odors she had never noticed when the old woman was home.

As she and Walker looked at the shelves of strange carvings, stuffed animals, and ancient pressed flowers, Mayra had a feeling that someone was watching them. She turned around several times, expecting to see Mrs. Cottler behind her. Of course no one was there.

Chill out, she told herself. But the strange feeling wouldn't go away.

"What's in there?" Walker asked, pointing to a doorway. "Is that a den?"

"No. It's her library."

"Let's take a look."

She followed him into the dark-paneled library with its floor-to-ceiling bookshelves on all four walls. An old mahogany desk and dark leather desk chair were the only pieces of furniture in the room. Mayra had only been in this room once or twice to pick up a book to read to Mrs. Cottler. She had never had an opportunity to explore it.

"Wow. Some of these books look really old," Walker said, looking up and down the shelves.

They began examining the titles. One wall contained shelf after shelf of classic novels, a set of Shakespeare, collections of Greek plays. "I wonder if she's read all of these," Walker said. "Hey, you've gotten really quiet. What's the matter?"

"I don't know. This is creepy," Mayra said. She turned and saw the cat standing in the doorway, staring at her with glowing yellow green eyes. She forced herself to turn back to the books. "Look at this, Walker."

He hurried over to her. "What have you found?"

"These books—look at the titles. They're all on witchcraft."

She read some of the titles aloud. Then she pulled out a book that looked really old. The heavy cover was torn and faded. She opened it up. The yellowed pages crumpled in her hand. "Look at this one." She held it up to him. The book was titled *The True Way of Worship*. There was a detailed engraving of a smiling devil on the first page.

"How old is that book?" Walker asked.

"There's no date," Mayra said. "But it looks really old. Look, it's filled with strange spells and recipes." She replaced the book on the shelf.

"This entire wall is all books about the occult," Walker said.

The cat meowed suddenly, startling Mayra. "Be quiet, Hazel," she called back to her. "We're only looking."

Turning to investigate a lower shelf, a title caught her eye. *Psychology of Sleepwalking*. She got down on her knees so she could examine the shelf more thoroughly. *The Sleepwalker. Sleepwalker Casebook.*

"She lied to me," Mayra said aloud.

"What? What are you doing down there?" Walker had a huge, leather-bound book the size of a dictionary in his arms.

"These are all books about sleepwalking."

He slammed the huge book shut. "Really?"

"After I sleepwalked for the first time, I asked Mrs. Cottler if she knew anything about sleepwalking, and all she said was, it's very mysterious."

"And she has a whole shelf on sleepwalking."

"She deliberately didn't want me to know that she knew about sleepwalking."

Walker helped her to her feet. "I'm beginning to think your theory is right," he said, not letting go of her hand. "Mrs. Cottler *must* be a witch. And look at that sleepwalking book—the yellow one—*Sleepwalker's Diary*. Look how it's sticking out."

"You mean it looks like it was recently used," Mayra said.

"Yes. It does."

Mayra pulled it out and set it on the table. "Maybe I'll borrow this one and read it later. Maybe I'll borrow a few of these."

Walker put his arms around her and pulled her into a warm hug.

"I'm so glad you're here," she said. "If I had come here by myself and found all this stuff, I would've freaked."

"It's a weird book collection," Walker said. "Definitely weird."

"Come on upstairs," Mayra said, pulling him by the hands. "I want to show you the black candles. Maybe there's more stuff up there."

They were nearly to the doorway when Mayra noticed the two photographs on the desk in the center of the room. "Oh, no!" she cried, pointing to the photos. "Walker—look! I don't believe it!"

chapter

14

The cat meowed angrily and leapt up onto the desktop. Mayra ignored her and picked up the photos, which were in a double frame. She held them up so Walker could see.

"It's Stephanie and Link," Walker said, looking as astonished as Mayra. "Those are their school photos from last year."

"What are they doing here on Mrs. Cottler's desk?" Mayra asked, staring hard at the photos as if they could give her an answer.

The cat flicked a paw at Mayra, just missing her arm.

"Hazel, what's wrong with you?" Mayra asked. "You don't want me to pick up these pictures? You want a little attention for yourself, is that it?"

The cat stared up at her blankly.

Mayra replaced the photos on the desk. "Maybe there are some answers to this mystery inside," she said. She pulled open the center desk drawer. It was filled with photos and papers and notebooks and cards.

"Walker, look at this." She had found another photo of Stephanie in the drawer. This one had to be at least two or three years old.

She continued shuffling through the drawer's contents.

"If you find a picture of *me* in there, don't tell me!" Walker said. He was making a joke, but his voice was tinged with fear.

Mayra pulled out a stack of photos and began going through them. "I wonder if I'll find a photo of Big Neck in here," she said.

"You mean that guy who followed you?"

"Yeah. Cal. He's tied up in this somehow. He's probably Mrs. Cottler's *son!*"

Mayra pulled out a birthday card and opened it up. "Well, well."

"What?"

"Listen to this. It says, 'Happy Birthday, Aunt Lucy. Love, Stephanie.'"

"Aunt Lucy?"

"Mrs. Cottler is Stephanie's aunt!" Mayra cried. "And Link's aunt! Of course! It was Stephanie who told me about this job! Funny she never mentioned that Mrs. Cottler was her aunt."

"Yeah. Funny," Walker agreed.

Mayra began tossing photos and papers back into the desk drawer. "And now maybe Stephanie and her aunt are working together. Maybe they're *both* casting their disgusting spells on me, making me sleepwalk, making me think I'm totally losing it!"

"Calm down, calm down," Walker said.

"My beads." Mayra suddenly remembered the beads. "I'm going to get my beads back. That's the first thing I'm going to do. Then I'm going to get my scarf back from Stephanie."

"Your scarf?"

"Yeah. Then I'm going to quit this job and stay as far away from Mrs. Cottler and her precious niece and nephew as I can!"

She slammed the drawer shut and, nearly tripping over the cat, hurried out of the library.

"Mayra—where are you going?" Walker sounded quite bewildered.

"I told you. Upstairs to get my beads."

She ran up the stairs, Hazel right behind her, protesting loudly. "Hazel—look out. I don't want to trip over you."

Down the long hall and into the bedroom with its two low dressers side by side. There was the little jewelry box on the edge of the dresser, right where Mayra had seen it last.

She hurried up to it and reached inside for her beads.

"Oh, no!"

The box was empty.

The beads were gone.

"Whoa! Slow down," Donna said. "I don't think any of this would make sense even if I *wasn't* on painkillers!"

Seeing Donna had been a bit of a shock at first for Mayra. She hadn't meant to gasp so loudly when she had walked in the door. But to see her friend in casts, completely immobilized, with those tubes stuck in her arms was too hard to take.

At least Donna sounded a little more like herself. And she had regained enough of her sense of humor to complain about the hospital food and complain about one of the nurses, who had accidentally sat on Donna's arm while giving her some pills!

Even though the two girls had never had any trouble in the past, Mayra soon found making conversation really awkward. She sat uncomfortably in the folding chair beside Donna's bed and tried to think of things to tell her about the outside world.

Finally she couldn't hold it in any longer. She told Donna about going to Mrs. Cottler's house with Walker the day before, and how she had proved that the old woman was a witch and that Stephanie, her niece, was probably a witch too.

"I've heard of jumping to conclusions," Donna said sarcastically, "but this is ridiculous!"

"What do you mean?"

"I mean, what exactly have you proved, Mayra? You've proved that Stephanie and Link are related to Mrs. Cottler. Well, Stephanie probably told you that when she told you about the job, and you just weren't listening or something. And what else have you proved? That Mrs. Cottler is very interested in witchcraft and stuff like that."

"But it all fits together," Mayra insisted, impatient with Donna's skepticism. "I didn't start sleepwalking until I started working for Mrs. Cottler. Until I left my beads at her house."

"Ohh," Donna moaned.

"What's the matter? You really think I'm being stupid?"

"No. I have an itch on my neck, and I can't scratch it."

Mayra laughed. She leaned over the bed and scratched Donna's neck for her. "Now aren't you glad I stopped by?" she asked.

"Listen, I know you're real upset about the sleep-walking and everything," Donna said, getting back to the subject. "But don't go off the deep end. This is the twentieth century, remember? People don't go around casting spells on other people."

"Walker says that they do. Walker says there are more covens now than in the sixteen hundreds."

Donna groaned again.

"Another itch?"

"No. I'm just really sleepy. I'm sorry. It's the pills, I guess. I have to go to sleep now. I just can't stay awake. We'll talk later, okay? I have plenty of time to think about it all. I'm sure the two of us can figure out what's going on." She yawned. "Thanks for coming, Mayra."

"I'll come again soon," Mayra said, getting up.

"You get some sleep too," Donna called after her.

"I wish I could," Mayra muttered, and suddenly feeling really depressed, she walked out of the room and down the harshly lit hospital corridor.

She was halfway home, sitting on the crowded afternoon Division Street bus, her forehead pressed against the window, when she got the idea to go to Stephanie's house and confront her.

She looked at her watch. It was nearly five o'clock. Stephanie would be home from her summer job by now. And Link probably wouldn't be home from his job yet. The perfect time.

She pulled the cord, waited for the bus to stop, and then got off. It was only a few blocks to Stephanie's house. The sun was pumpkin orange, low in the sky. The evening air was cool and dry.

Mayra took a deep breath. What shall I say to her?

I'll just tell her point-blank that I know what's going on.

Of course she'll deny it. She'll deny everything.

But then I'll tell her what I saw at Mrs. Cottler's house. I'll tell her I know that the old witch is her aunt.

And I'll tell her that I know why she took my white scarf.

And then what?

And then she'll have to stop. She and the old woman will have to stop what they're doing to me.

One block to go. A yapping dog came running down a long, flat lawn toward her. It yipped in surprise when it reached the end of its chain and flipped over onto its back.

Mayra had to laugh. Dogs are so stupid, she thought.

Hazel flashed into her mind. That cat, on the other hand, seemed much too smart. Hazel certainly didn't like Mayra and Walker snooping about the house. The cat seemed positively relieved when the two of them had left. What a weird animal . . .

Now Mayra stood on Stephanie's front porch. The

front door was open. She peered through the screen door.

I can't wait for Stephanie to pull her "Miss Innocent" act on me, she thought. For once, I know too much for her to get away with it.

"Anybody home?" she called into the house.

No reply.

"Stephanie—are you home?"

Still silence.

Mayra pulled open the screen door and stepped into the front entranceway. She looked around the living room. It was strange being back in this house. Everything was so familiar. Not a thing had changed in it, and yet it seemed to Mayra as if she hadn't been there in ages.

"Stephanie?" she called upstairs.

Looking up to the top landing, she could see that Stephanie's door was closed. Maybe she's up in her room and can't hear me, she thought.

Climbing the thickly carpeted stairs, Mayra realized that her heart was pounding. This wasn't going to be pleasant. Maybe she should turn around and forget about it. She really hated confrontations of any sort.

No.

She had to go through with it. She couldn't take many more nights of being afraid to go to sleep, afraid that she would have that awful dream and wake up somewhere far from her house.

She knocked on Stephanie's bedroom door.

No reply. But she could hear some sort of music inside.

"Stephanie? Are you in there?"

She pushed open the door and peered in.

The room was dark except for the light of three flickering candles. There in the darkness was Stephanie, her back to Mayra, down on the floor beside the candles. She was sitting cross-legged in front of a white circle, and she was chanting the same three or four words over and over again in a near-tuneless melody. There were several small items inside the circle. But in the dim, flickering light, Mayra couldn't make out what they were.

One thing, however, she could make out very clearly—Stephanie had Mayra's white scarf tied around her head.

chapter

15

Stephanie suddenly stopped chanting and turned around. "Mayra—what are you doing *here?*"

"Never mind that. What are *you* doing?" Mayra asked, stepping into the room.

Stephanie jumped to her feet. "Just practicing. Who let you in? Is my mom home?"

"I let myself in," Mayra said.

"You can let yourself out," Stephanie snapped. Her green eyes flared in the candlelight, much like Hazel's eyes.

"Not until you tell me why you're doing this," Mayra said, standing her ground.

"Doing this? What do you mean?"

Mayra pointed to the circle. Standing closer, she could see that there were bones inside it, chicken bones probably, arranged in triangles.

"You know I've always been interested in the occult," Stephanie said. She flicked on the dresser lamp. "So I'm just fooling around. What's the big deal?"

"Why are you casting a spell on me?" The words just fell out of Mayra's mouth. She hadn't really planned to ask that question. Now that she had, she suddenly felt embarrassed.

Stephanie laughed. "Cut me some slack, Mayra. Are you losing it altogether?"

"You *are* casting a spell on me," Mayra insisted. "You're wearing my scarf."

"Huh?"

Stephanie reached up and pulled off the white scarf, releasing her black hair, which tumbled down her shoulders. "Here." She pushed it into Mayra's hands. "Take it."

"You were using it for your spell," Mayra repeated, starting to feel doubtful.

"I was using it to hold up my hair," Stephanie said, sneering. "I washed my hair when I got home from work. I wanted to keep it off my shoulders. Take your stupid scarf."

"But, Stephanie, I know everything," Mayra said, trying to keep her voice normal, suddenly feeling as if she wanted to run, run from this house and never see Stephanie or her brother again. "I know that Mrs. Cottler is your aunt."

"Boy, is that a hot flash," Stephanie scoffed, dropping down onto the edge of her bed. "Of *course* you know Mrs. Cottler is my aunt. I told you she was when I told you about the job."

"No, you didn't," Mayra said. She thought hard. Was Stephanie telling the truth? Had she told Mayra?

Mayra couldn't remember. "I'm sure you didn't," she said.

I never should've started this, Mayra thought. I felt so certain about everything when I came up here and found Stephanie chanting on the floor. But now . . .

No. I am right. I *have* to be right.

I'm not making all this up. I *am* sleepwalking because someone is casting a spell on me. If it isn't Stephanie, it's her aunt.

Stephanie's lying, Mayra decided.

"Do you think other people are out to get you too?" Stephanie asked, crossing her arms tightly over her chest.

"Why are you being so mean to me?" Mayra blurted out. "I thought we were friends."

"I'm not being mean to you. I'm angry because you burst into my room and started making crazy accusations. *You're* the one who's being mean. You're the one who accused me of casting a spell on you, of all the crazy things!"

"I'm not crazy!" Mayra exclaimed. "Do you know someone named Cal?"

"Who?"

"Cal. I don't know his last name. A big blond guy with a huge neck."

Stephanie laughed. "No. I don't know him. Why should I know him?"

"Your aunt knows him. Your aunt sent him after me."

"Mayra, I really don't know what you're talking about. You haven't made any sense at all since you barged in here. Are you feeling okay? You look so tired and awful."

"You *know* I haven't been sleeping well!" Mayra cried, feeling herself start to lose control and unable to do anything about it. "You know I've been sleepwalking—and you know why!"

"Sleepwalking?"

I knew she'd play innocent, Mayra thought.

"Maybe you're sleepwalking because you have a guilty conscience for dumping Link."

"Stephanie, come off it."

"Come off it? You're the one who started it, Mayra. You know what I thought when I first saw you standing here?"

"What?"

"I thought you had come to make up with Link since Walker dropped you."

Mayra suddenly felt cold all over, as if her blood had frozen in her veins. What was Stephanie saying? Mayra didn't think she had heard right.

"Since Walker dropped you."

What could Stephanie mean? Maybe I *am* cracking up, Mayra thought.

"Walker? Dropped me? Huh?"

"Everyone knows he's going with Suki Thomas now."

Have I stepped into the Twilight Zone? Mayra thought.

"Now you're just being vicious," Mayra said softly, starting to back out of the room.

"I am not," Stephanie insisted. "Don't tell me you didn't know."

"There's nothing to know. I was with Walker this morning. You're just making this up to hurt me."

"I saw Walker and Suki having pizza at the mall," Stephanie said.

"Well, so did I. Big deal. That doesn't mean Walker has dropped me." Mayra clutched the white scarf tightly in her hand, so tightly it hurt. "That's just so babyish of you," Mayra said, her voice trembling.

Stephanie didn't say anything, just shrugged and rolled her eyes.

"Goodbye, Stephanie. Sorry I barged in on your spell-casting." Mayra turned quickly and headed out the door, feeling a little dizzy.

"I'm sorry too!" Stephanie called after her.

Then suddenly, as Mayra reached the stairs, Stephanie was right behind her. She put a hand on Mayra's shoulder. "I really am sorry," she said softly, with no trace of anger. "Sorry about . . . everything."

Mayra flung herself down the stairs, pushed open the screen door, and ran outside, gasping for air. The sun was nearly down, but the air was still hot and humid. She stood in the middle of the gravel drive, breathing hard, waiting to feel a little better.

What did Stephanie mean when she said she was "sorry about *everything*"? Mayra wondered.

Sorry about being so mean?

Sorry about casting the sleepwalking spell?

Sorry about making up that horrible lie about Walker?

She didn't have long to think about it. She looked up to see Link's red pickup truck pulling up the drive.

"Hey—Mayra—hi!"

"Oh, no," Mayra muttered. Link was about the *last* person she wanted to see at that moment.

He pulled the truck to a stop a few feet in front of

her and jumped out, a wide grin on his handsome face. "This is a surprise."

"I was—uh—talking to Stephanie."

His grin faded. "Really?"

The truck.

She suddenly remembered the truck. Donna. The madman who crashed into her.

"Link," she started, "two days ago, did you—"

She looked down to examine the truck's bumper. It was smooth and undented. She examined both front fenders. They were flawless, like new.

It wasn't Link, she thought.

How could I have ever thought it was Link?

Maybe Stephanie is right. Maybe I *am* cracking up. I'm suspecting everyone I know of being out to get me.

But then she thought of Donna lying in the hospital bed with the tubes in her arm. And of Cal, who glared at her with such menace. And of sleepwalking into the woods . . .

"I'm not crazy," she said, without realizing she was speaking aloud.

Link stared at her in surprise.

chapter

16

*T*hat night she had the dream again.

This time the wind howled as she stepped onto the lake. Dark waves, the color of ink, tossed about her ankles, soaked the hem of her nightgown.

The colors were so vivid. The night sky was like black velvet. The moon golden, nearly as bright as the sun.

She walked over the waves. The water felt cold, so cold on her feet.

Again, someone was watching her from the shore.

Who was it? She wanted desperately to see.

She tried to turn around, but something held her back. She had to keep walking, walking so slowly but steadily on top of the lapping, dark waves.

Soon she would be surrounded by water. The land, the woods, would all disappear behind her.

Who was it? Who was it behind her on the shore?

Who was watching her so silently as she walked over the water?

Suddenly she could see. Everything shifted, and she could see the shore, the low scrub, the hunkering dark trees behind it.

It was so bright now. The moon was blindingly white. It spread over the shore like a spotlight.

Who was there? Someone was standing in that white light.

She squinted to see better.

Yes. Yes. She could see him now.

It was Walker.

Walker, standing so statue-still, so silent, watching her as she turned once again and walked over the low waves.

Walker, why are you watching me like that?

Then, suddenly, he was gone with the bright moonlight. It was replaced by the wet darkness of the waves. They were pulling her down, down.

She tried to resist, tried to swim. But the water was too powerful. It was up to the waist of her nightgown, so cold now, so freezing cold and so heavy.

Heavy, heavier. She was sinking into the water.

Oh, help me, somebody. Why can't I swim? Why can't I break away?

Down she fell. She tried to raise her arms as her head went under, but she couldn't lift them from her side.

Down into the heavy, dark water. It was choking her now.

Oh, let me breathe.

She woke up.

But she was still in the dream.

Or so it seemed.

"Oh, let me breathe."

The water choked her. She gasped and struggled against the waves. She flailed her arms, and gasped, swallowing more water.

Was she still asleep?

No. This was real. She was in water. Deep water.

She was drowning.

The water swelled over her head.

She closed her eyes and struggled back up to the top.

She burst above the surface, choking, splashing, reaching up, trying to pull herself up, pull herself out of the water, of the dream that wasn't a dream.

She tried to scream, to cry for help. But no sound came out. Her hair was tangled, matted over her face. She struggled to push it away so she could breathe.

I can't stay up, she thought, and started to drop again, her eyes opened wide, her heart pounding, the only sound except for the quiet, deadly swirling of the waters as they encircled her once again.

I'm drowning.

I'm dead.

But where am I?

She started to see colors, bright colors.

Her chest hurt. Her lungs felt ready to explode.

I'm drowning.

I'm dead.

Strong arms grabbed her shoulders. Strong arms hoisted her up.

Was she dreaming this too?

She opened her eyes. No. There was a small speedboat. And a man in a baseball cap pulled down over his forehead. The man had a short beard.

He had her by the shoulders. He pulled. She was heavy now, as heavy as a whale.

"Help me," he said. "Can you help me lift you?" His voice sounded so far away, miles away.

He pulled again. She couldn't help him. The small boat tilted and bobbed.

It seemed like forever until she was sprawled in the small boat.

"Can you talk?" he asked. He had kind eyes beneath the baseball cap.

She raised her head and vomited. Water poured out of her mouth, the brackish lake water. She choked, took a deep breath, vomited again, began to feel better.

"Can you breathe?" he asked.

She saw a rod and reel, a tackle box beside the small outboard motor at the back of the boat.

He didn't wait for an answer. "Good thing I came along."

She nodded. She started to shake. "It-it's so cold," she said.

He tugged the rope on the motor and it started right up. "I'll get you to shore," he said. "Sorry I don't have a blanket. I didn't expect to fish a girl out of the lake tonight. You're the only thing I caught, though."

Mayra looked to the dark, tree-lined shore. They were nearly there. She hadn't sleepwalked very far into the lake. Just far enough to drown herself.

"What were you doing in the water this time of night all by yourself?" the fisherman asked.

"I don't know," she said.

chapter

17

Mrs. Barnes, biting her lower lip, put down the phone receiver. "Dr. Sterne says he can see you in the morning. Would you like another bowl of tomato soup?"

"No. I'm warmed up," Mayra said, twirling the soup spoon around and around between her fingers. "Do you really think he can help me?"

Her mother walked across the kitchen, came up behind her, and put her arms around Mayra's shoulders. "Mayra, we've got to do *something*. You nearly drowned tonight." She bent down and pressed her cheek against Mayra's still-wet hair. "I really do think Dr. Sterne can help."

Mayra sighed. She looked up at the kitchen clock. Was it really three-thirty in the morning?

"You'd better go to bed," her mother said. "Think you can sleep?"

"I don't know if I *want* to sleep," Mayra said. She

stared out the window into the darkness. "I'm really scared, Mom. Why am I doing this?"

"Don't worry. Dr. Sterne will help you find out why, and in the meantime you can sleep in my room," Mrs. Barnes said, but her trembling lower lip and the tears forming in the corners of her eyes told Mayra that her mother was as frightened and mystified by this as she was.

The two hospital receptionists, seated inside the circular desk in the center of the lobby, were more interested in talking to each other than to the people who came up to them asking for directions and information. "I don't know, Barbara. I just don't know," the smaller woman kept repeating to the larger woman, who kept shaking her head in agreement.

Mayra, dressed in tan shorts and a long-sleeved, yellow T-shirt, waited patiently, leaning on the desk. After a while she realized she'd have to interrupt if she was ever going to get to Dr. Sterne's office in time. "Can you tell me how to get to Dr. Sterne's office?"

"Fourth floor," the one named Barbara said without really acknowledging Mayra's presence.

"Take the elevators on the left," her companion added, surprisingly helpful.

Mayra thanked them and headed to the left bank of elevators. Even though it was before nine in the morning, a large crowd was waiting for the next elevator.

"Oh. Sorry!" Mayra bumped into a woman with a big white cast on her foot.

"Watch it." The woman glared at Mayra and moved away, leaning heavily on a metal crutch.

I'm so nervous, I'm not paying attention to anything, Mayra thought. I don't want to be here. I'm not sick. Why am I in the hospital?

She wondered where her mother was. Probably on the sixth floor. That was the recovery floor. Mrs. Barnes had wanted to accompany Mayra to Dr. Sterne's office, but she had an overload of demanding patients to deal with up there.

Why do they keep it so hot in here? Mayra wondered. She pushed her hair back off her shoulder, wishing she had pinned it up.

The elevator finally arrived and everyone crushed into it, looking very sour and uncomfortable. On the second floor two doctors in green surgical suits and caps got on, talking to each other in low voices about a patient.

By the time the elevator reached the fourth floor, Mayra was crushed against the back wall. "Getting out!" she called. But no one seemed to hear her. "Please—getting out."

The doors started to close as she pushed her way to the front of the elevator. She made a desperate leap and popped out just as the doors slammed shut.

Now where do I go? she asked herself. She searched the pale green walls until she found a sign. PSYCHIATRIC. It had an arrow beside it, pointing to the right, so Mayra walked to the right, passed through two swinging doors, and kept walking.

There were patients' rooms on both sides of the narrow hallway. Through half-closed doors, she could see people lying in their beds. Some were sleeping.

Some were awake, staring up at TV sets that seemed to be suspended from the ceiling. The sounds of a game show echoed through the halls.

I must have made a wrong turn, Mayra thought. These people look sick. They don't look like psychiatric patients.

"Can I help you?" A large orderly carrying a stack of trays stepped in front of her.

"Oh. Yes. I'm looking for Dr. Sterne's office."

"He's in Psychiatric."

"Yeah. I know. I—"

"Just turn around, go back through those doors, and make a sharp right."

"Okay. Thanks a lot." She turned around uncertainly and tried to follow his directions.

Past the doors she turned right and headed down a similar hall, this one with pale blue walls. "I've got to get out of here," Mayra said aloud.

She turned again and walked quickly through another set of swinging doors. Another sign said PSYCHIATRIC. An arrow pointed straight ahead. A nurse pushing a cart of breakfast trays smiled reassuringly at her as she passed.

Feeling a little encouraged, Mayra continued walking, reading the nameplates beside each door. She reached a small nurses' station where a tired-looking nurse was slumped behind a desk, her eyes closed.

Mayra was about to ask her the location of Dr. Sterne's office when she stopped—and gasped aloud.

The man there . . .

It was Cal.

She recognized the short blond hair. The staring eyes. The wide neck.

He didn't see her at first. He was sitting on a couch near the nurses' station, his eyes on the sign that said PSYCHIATRIC.

But then he turned and looked at her, and their eyes met.

Mayra quickly looked down, saw the cardboard bracelet on his arm.

Oh, no! she thought, realizing at once why Cal was there.

He was a mental patient!

chapter

18

"Hey—you!" It took Cal a while to recognize her. He seemed confused, groggy. He struggled to his feet, and Mayra saw for the first time that he was gripping a cane.

Mayra turned, looking for a place to run.

His face reddened. His expression turned from surprise to anger. "Hey—stop!"

His shouts woke up the nurse, who leapt from her chair. Keeping the nurse's desk between them, Mayra walked quickly away.

"Hey—stop!"

He was coming after her, his face red, his eyes bulging with anger.

Mayra started to jog. She almost collided with a cart of lunch trays. "Hey—watch where you're going!" an alarmed orderly called.

She looked back. Cal was gaining on her, leaning on his cane as he lumbered forward, waving his free hand at her frantically.

"Stop—you! Somebody stop that girl!" he bellowed.

She turned a corner, looking for a place to hide. She ducked into a room. "Hello? Can I help you?" A young woman sat up quickly in her bed near the window.

"Oh. Sorry. Wrong room," Mayra said. She slipped back out into the hallway.

"Gotcha now!" Cal yelled, coming around the corner. "Stop. You won't get away!"

"What do you want? Leave me alone!" Mayra cried.

Cal lunged forward clumsily, desperate to get to her. Suddenly two nurses appeared on either side of him, grabbing him, holding him back. "Idiots! Let me go!" he bellowed.

Then Mayra saw the sign next to an open door: DR. LAWRENCE STERNE. A young man with curly copper hair stood outside the door. He was dressed in a dark brown suit and was sifting through some papers on a clipboard.

Hearing Cal struggle noisily with the nurses, Mayra darted around the young man and plunged into the empty office. She started to close the door behind her, but the young man held up the clipboard to block the door.

"Excuse me, miss," he said, looking very surprised. "What are you doing?"

"I'm—uh—I have an appointment with Dr. Sterne," Mayra stammered. "This is his office, right?"

"Yes, it is." He followed her into the office and placed his clipboard on his cluttered desk. "I'm Doctor Sterne."

"But you're too young!"

That's what Mayra almost blurted out. Somehow she managed to stop herself in time. But she wasn't able to stop her mouth from dropping open in surprise.

"I'm not at all what you pictured, right?" Dr. Sterne said, looking her up and down.

"Well, yes," Mayra admitted.

"I've tried to grow a beard so that I'll look older," the psychiatrist said, "but it comes in all splotchy. Makes me look like a ferret." He smiled at her, but his expression quickly changed. "Why did you run in here like that?"

"A man was chasing me. One of the mental patients."

"Mental patient?" Dr. Sterne stepped out into the hall and looked both ways.

"He's big and blond. He has a huge neck."

"A huge neck?" he called from the hallway. "Ella? Did you see someone out here with a huge neck?"

A tall, thin nurse with straight black hair and black horn-rimmed glasses appeared in the hallway beside Dr. Sterne. She wasn't the same nurse that had helped Mayra escape by restraining Cal.

"No, I haven't seen anyone," the nurse said. "Was he a patient of yours?"

"No. No. Thanks," Dr. Sterne said, rubbing his chin. He returned to the office, staring skeptically at Mayra.

"He really was there," Mayra said. "He's chased me before."

"The man with the huge neck?"

"Yes. He asked my friend about me. And he followed me one day. And now I found out that he's a mental patient here and—"

Dr. Sterne held both hands up. "Whoa. Slow down. Let me get this straight. You say a man with a huge neck has been following you outside even though he's a patient in this hospital?"

"Yes. You don't believe me, do you?" Mayra asked, suddenly feeling angry.

"I just realized who you are," he said, sitting down in the tall, black leather chair behind his cluttered desk. "You're Amy Barnes's daughter. Mayra, right?"

Mayra felt herself blushing for some reason. This man was her mother's friend, and now he thought she was totally bananas, imagining that people were following her.

"Yes. Mom said—"

"That you've been sleepwalking."

"She told you the whole story?"

"Yes. But I'd like to hear it in your words." He motioned for her to sit down in the green leather armchair across from his desk.

"Aren't I supposed to lie down on a couch or something?"

"I'm supposed to be a bald, old man with a foreign accent, and you're supposed to lie down on a couch," he said, chuckling. "Well, sorry. I don't have an accent, and I don't have a couch. Think you can talk to me sitting up?"

Mayra smiled for the first time. At least he had a sense of humor. She plopped down in the chair and let out a long sigh.

"Are you frightened?" Dr. Sterne asked, leaning forward over his desk. He turned down a fresh sheet of paper on a long yellow pad.

"No. I mean, yes. I mean, not of you."

He looked disappointed. "You don't think I'm a scary guy?"

"Not too," Mayra said. "You're trying to be real sweet to put me at ease, right?"

"Right," he agreed quickly. "Want to see me juggle three apples?"

Mayra laughed. "No. Not really. I'm feeling better now. Really."

"You look kinda tired," he said. "Have you been getting much sleep?"

"No. I'm afraid to go to sleep."

"Afraid you'll sleepwalk?"

"Yes."

"Start at the beginning," he said, making a note on the pad. "Tell me about the first time you sleepwalked. Every detail you can remember. Re-create it all for me. Close your eyes if you want to. Try to picture everything you tell me."

Mayra closed her eyes, but quickly reopened them. "No. I might fall asleep." Staring past him to the window behind his desk, Mayra proceeded to tell him as much as she could, starting out with the strange dream she had had each time.

It took a long time to tell it all. By the time she finished recounting being pulled out of the lake, choking and nearly half drowned, he had filled the entire page of the notepad.

"Am I cracking up or what?" Mayra asked, surprised that her voice was trembling. She thought she would feel relieved after telling her story to a psychiatrist, but she found herself feeling more nervous and frightened than ever.

"You're not cracking up," Dr. Sterne said, making a face. "Stop thinking that way. I think something is troubling you, troubling you deeply. But I don't think you need to worry about having some sort of mental breakdown. That's not what causes your sleepwalking."

"Then what *does* cause it?" Mayra demanded.

"I think it could be caused by repressed trauma," Dr. Sterne said.

"What? You'll have to explain that. I haven't taken psych in school yet."

"Something is troubling you," he explained. "Something very upsetting. You're trying to deal with it when you're asleep because you find it too upsetting to deal with when you're awake."

Mayra stared at him, thinking about what he was suggesting. "Something very upsetting is troubling me?"

He nodded. "Your subconscious is trying to work it out."

"But if it's so upsetting, wouldn't I remember what it is?"

He opened his desk drawer, searched quickly for something, then reclosed it. He stared into her eyes. "Do you have any idea what it might be?"

Mayra shook her head. "No. I can't think of anything that's upsetting me that much. I don't like my summer job very much, but that's no big deal." Mayra realized she hadn't told Dr. Sterne about Mrs. Cottler, or about her suspicions that Mrs. Cottler—or Stephanie—had cast a sleepwalking spell on her.

If I did, he would *really* think I'm crazy, she reasoned.

"I broke up with my boyfriend a while ago. But I'm not too upset about that either. I have a new boyfriend."

Dr. Sterne looked at his watch. "Oh, I'm really sorry. That's all the time we have for today," he said.

Mayra stood up. "Sorry. I—"

"I want you to come back next week," he said. He stood up and guided her to the door. "Do you want to come back and talk some more?"

"I—I guess."

"And I don't want you to worry that you're losing your mind or are desperately sick or something. Wait a second." He walked back to his desk and scribbled something on a pad. He tore off the sheet and gave it to her.

"What's this?" Mayra couldn't read a word of it.

"It's a prescription. For something to help you sleep. It's very mild. Nonaddictive. I want you to take it every night a half hour before you go to bed. I've had real success with it. Another patient of mine was a sleepwalker, and this drug stopped the sleepwalking for good."

"But I—"

"You need to sleep. You're really overtired, Mayra. And I think that if you could get yourself into a more tranquil frame of mind, then maybe you could start to discover what is really troubling you, the true cause of your sleepwalking."

Mayra tucked the prescription into the pocket of her shorts. "So that's your advice? Get some sleep?"

He smiled. "At least I didn't say, 'Take two aspirin and call me in the morning.'"

"You look a lot better today," Mayra told Donna, dropping wearily onto the folding chair beside Donna's hospital bed.

"You mean I'm semiconscious instead of unconscious?"

"I mean you look better. For one thing, those awful tubes are gone."

"Yeah. I'm on my own now," Donna said sarcastically. "I'm not Frankenstein anymore. Now I'm just the Mummy. Look at these bandages!"

Mayra felt a chill go down her back. It should be me lying in that hospital bed, she thought. It was supposed to be me. The maniac in the pickup truck—he thought he was pushing *me* off the road.

"So tell me some news of the outside world," Donna said.

Mayra was thinking about Dr. Sterne, about his explanation of her sleepwalking. Something was troubling her, he had said. Something was troubling her so much that she couldn't think about it while she was awake.

What could it possibly be?

"Hey, Mayra—did you conk out?" Donna's voice interrupted her thoughts.

"Oh. Sorry."

"What's happening with your job? Do you still think Mrs. Cottler is casting a spell on you?"

"Yes," Mayra answered quickly. "I mean no. I mean I don't know."

"Well, at least you're clear about it." Donna laughed. "Ouch! Don't make me laugh. It's too painful."

"I sleepwalked again," Mayra said, suddenly feeling very weary. "This time I almost drowned."

"Oh, no. Mayra, I'm sorry. Where were you?"

"In the lake. Behind the Fear Street woods. You know, near Mrs. Cottler's house."

"You walked all the way there in your sleep?"

"Yeah. First I dream about the lake, then I walk to it. It's so strange. You know, Mrs. Cottler lost a child in the lake. I wonder if that has anything to do with . . ." Her mind drifted off. She didn't finish her thought.

"What happened when you got to the lake?" Donna asked.

"When I got there, I guess I kept walking."

"And you didn't wake up in the water?" Donna's face filled with horror and concern.

"No. Not until some fisherman came by and pulled me out. If he hadn't been there, I—"

Donna reached over and grabbed Mayra's hand with her one free hand. "Mayra, you've got to tell someone about Mrs. Cottler. You've got to tell someone what you suspect."

"I've just been to a shrink downstairs. That's why I'm here so early."

"And you told him—"

"No, I couldn't. I don't think shrinks believe in witchcraft, do you?"

"No, I guess not. But, Mayra, this is so scary. The next time . . ."

Mayra let go of Donna's hand and walked to the window. She stared down at the crowded parking lot, thinking hard.

The lake.

She had to think about the lake. All this time she'd been focusing on everything but the lake. But the lake now seemed so important.

The lake had to be a clue to why this was happening to her, why she was sleepwalking.

There was something troubling her, Dr. Sterne had said. Something troubling her that she was trying to solve in her sleep.

Something troubling her . . . *about the lake.*

"I'm going to do something about it," she blurted out, not realizing she was talking aloud.

"Huh?" Donna called from the bed. "Mayra, come back. I can't see you."

"I'm going to go to the lake."

"What are you talking about?"

"I'm going to the lake. Tonight."

"Terrific. Have a nice time," Donna said, confused.

"I'm always going there in my sleep. Tonight I'll go there while I'm awake. Maybe I'll learn something that way, Donna. Maybe the lake will tell me something."

"The lake will tell you something?" Donna looked even more confused.

"I'll let you know," Mayra said, very excited. "Talk to you later."

"Fine," Donna said dejectedly, watching her friend hurry away. "I'll be here. I'm not going anywhere."

* * *

The night air was hot and sticky. Tree toads chirped relentlessly in the trees. Somewhere far off in the woods, a dog howled mournfully, waited for a reply, then howled again.

"Ow!" Mayra slapped at a mosquito. She looked up at the dark trees, so still, still as a photograph. She stepped deeper into the Fear Street woods, her flashlight aimed at the narrow, weed-clotted path in front of her.

"I'm *glad* Walker didn't come," she told herself. She pulled a clump of tall weeds out of her way.

She had called him right after dinner and asked if he wanted to come with her to the lake. "The lake? What for?" He had sounded terribly confused.

"Just for fun," she said, not wanting to reveal the true purpose of the journey over the phone. After all, she wasn't really sure why she was going. She just knew she had to do *something*.

"Walking through the Fear Street woods at night doesn't sound like fun to me," Walker said.

"But the lake will be so pretty tonight," she argued. "It's nearly a full moon."

"I can't, Mayra. I promised my cousin I'd baby-sit for her twins tonight."

"You sure?" Mayra asked suspiciously.

"Really. I'd come with you if I could. Listen—we'll go to the lake some other time, okay?"

"Well . . ."

"You wouldn't go by yourself, would you?"

"Well . . ."

"No. Really. I don't want you to go by yourself. That's just not smart."

"Well . . ."

"Mayra? Come on. I'll worry about you too much."

She debated in her mind whether to tell him the real reason she wanted to go to the lake at night, and decided he really wouldn't understand. "I'll call you later," she had told him, "to see how you're surviving with your cousin's twin terrors." Then she hung up.

At first she was disappointed that Walker couldn't come with her. But then she realized she was better off without him. If there was something she had to discover at the lake, she probably stood a better chance of finding it alone.

Moonlight filtered eerily through the thick trees. Glimmers of silver light made the woods seem unreal, like a place in a dark fairy tale. The air was so still, Mayra could hear her every breath. The tree toads suddenly stopped chirping. Now the only other sounds were those of her sneakers scraping the soft ground as she made her way along the winding path through the woods.

The fear came over her all at once, as if sneaking up from behind and pouncing on her.

She stopped and tried to shake it off.

But she was trembling all over. Her legs felt weak as paper. Her head was pounding.

What is happening to me? she wondered.

Maybe it was the realization that she was all alone in the Fear Street woods, where so many horrible and mysterious things had taken place.

Maybe it was being so close to the lake where she had nearly been swallowed up the night before.

Maybe Mrs. Cottler was working her evil magic, using her witch's powers to keep Mayra from the lake, to keep Mayra from discovering what she had to discover.

I've got to keep going, Mayra thought.

She directed the flashlight along the path and started walking again, forcing her legs forward, forcing herself to ignore her trembling body, her throbbing forehead.

After a short while the lake came into view. It was steel gray under the dark sky. The water lapped gently, almost silently against the muddy shore.

Glad to be out of the woods, Mayra started to run over the tall grass that led toward the water.

The lake seemed larger than usual, so wide it disappeared into the darkness on both sides. Fear Island, the small island in the center of the lake, was just a bulging shadow in the distance.

Mayra took a deep breath.

What secret do you have for me, lake?

Why do I dream about you? Why do I keep walking to you in my sleep?

Why does Mrs. Cottler draw me to you?

What awful secret are you hiding from me?

She sat down on the edge of a small wooden dock that jutted out a few yards over the water. The fear hadn't left her, but the trembling had stopped.

The water below was so beautiful, so soothing.

She was about to take her sneakers off and dip her feet in the water when she heard the footsteps on the grass behind her, and realized she was no longer alone.

chapter

19

"**W**ho's there?"

Mayra's voice came out a whisper. Her body seemed to freeze. She had to force herself to breathe.

She had one sneaker on, one off. Struggling to put the sneaker back on, she stared into the darkness.

"Who's there?"

The sneaker was knotted. She couldn't get it back on. And her hands were shaking too hard to untie the knot.

She hopped off the dock, holding the sneaker in one hand, and looked for a place to hide. There was a clump of low shrubs a few hundred feet down the shoreline.

She heard the crack of twigs. Footsteps on the soft ground.

"Who is it?" she called, not recognizing her voice, her throat choked with fear.

More footsteps, growing louder. Then— "Hey!" a voice called.

It was too late to run.

"Hey!" A familiar voice.

Her heart was pounding. She raised the sneaker high as if to use it as a weapon.

He appeared suddenly, stepping out of the darkness and into the silvery metal light of the moon.

"Link!"

"Hi, Mayra."

"Link! What are you doing here?"

"I saw you. On Fear Street. I was in the truck. I decided to follow. I was worried. I mean, what are you doing here all alone?"

"What business is it of yours?"

For a brief second she was glad to see him. But when he mentioned the truck, she froze.

She pictured Donna lying in the hospital, tubes in her arm.

The fear returned. The trembling. The headache. She decided to cover it up by being angry. She wouldn't let him see that she was frightened.

"Are you sleepwalking again?" Link asked, an odd half smile forming on his face.

"No, I am not," she said coldly. "How do you know about that, anyway?"

He shrugged. The half smile faded. His dark eyes burned into hers. "You shouldn't be alone in the Fear Street woods, Mayra. You've lived in Shadyside long enough to know that." Did he sound sincerely concerned? Or was that some kind of veiled threat?

"I can take care of myself," she said, turning her back on him. She sat back down on the tree stump and struggled to untie the knot from her sneaker. "I'm sick of you following me around. I want you to stop it—starting now."

"But I really am worried about you, Mayra."

"Well, go worry somewhere else," she snapped. She turned to look up at him. His face was filled with concern.

"You shouldn't be here," he repeated, ignoring her anger.

"I'm meeting Walker," she lied. "I wish you wouldn't be here when he gets here."

"You're meeting him here?"

"Yeah. Is that okay with you?"

He laughed.

"What's so funny?"

"This isn't exactly a convenient meeting place, is it? Look around. You don't see a whole lot of couples walking through the woods in the dark to meet here."

"Well—Walker and I like a little excitement." She knew that sounded lame, but it was the best she could do.

He frowned and tossed his dark mane of hair as if shaking off her words.

"How come you two didn't come here together?" Link asked.

"Go away, Link. I really want to be alone here."

"Mayra, I'm sorry. Really. I was in the truck back on Fear Street, and I saw you. I shouldn't have followed you, but—I don't know."

"Did you have the truck on the highway, Link? Between here and Waynesbridge?" The question just popped out. She had to know the answer. She had to know if it was his pickup that nearly killed Donna.

"Huh?"

"You heard me. Last week. Were you the one?"

"Mayra, what are you talking about?"

She stared into his dark eyes, searching for the truth.

"A red pickup truck tried to run Donna off the highway. She was driving my mother's Toyota and—"

He looked genuinely confused. "Donna? Is she okay? Mayra, are *you* feeling all right? You're not making any sense."

She shook her head. She couldn't tell if Link was pretending not to know anything or if he was really innocent. If it was his truck on the highway, he'd never admit it now, she realized. She was sorry she had asked him about it.

Suddenly he reached down and grabbed her arm. "Mayra—let me take you home."

She jumped to her feet and pulled away from his grasp. "Let go of me!"

"I miss you so much," he said. He moved forward and grabbed her with both arms.

Mayra tried to pull away, but he was holding her too tightly. His dark eyes were wild. "I miss you so much," he repeated. His voice sounded tense, strange.

He's out of control, Mayra thought.

"Link—let go of me!"

"No!" he cried. "I won't!" He tightened his grip, pulling her against him. "Not till you admit that you miss me too!"

He dropped his arms around her waist.

"Link—no!"

He squeezed her tightly. He lowered his face to kiss her.

"No—Link. Please!"

She turned her head. He pressed his face against her cheek.

"Let go of me!"

She raised a fist and hit his left ear.

He jerked up his head, startled. "Hey—"

She ducked down quickly, surprising him, pulling out of his grasp.

"Mayra, wait—"

She scrambled toward the dock, turned, and saw him reaching out for her.

"Wait—I didn't mean anything—" he called, his eyes frantic and wild.

Thinking only of escape, she plunged off the dock and into the water.

Oh! So cold!

She gasped, momentarily paralyzed by the shock of the cold.

And at that moment it came back to her. . . .

chapter
20

*I*t all came back to her.

That night of horrors, more than a month before.

The shock of the water brought it all back. And as she struggled back to shore, she suddenly remembered everything.

And she heard the terrifying screams all over again.

"Mayra—what's the matter?" Link cried, seeing the expression on her face, seeing her cover her ears with her hands as she tried to shut out the newly remembered screams that wouldn't go away.

"Take me home," she managed to say. "Just take me home."

He helped her back through the woods to Fear Street. Then she collapsed into the front seat of the truck, and he drove her home in silence.

When she got to her house, she didn't remember the ride. She didn't remember saying good night to Link. She didn't remember climbing the stairs to her room, undressing, and getting into bed.

She was reliving that Saturday night, lost in it, still feeling the excitement, the excitement that so quickly turned into a nightmare.

Once again she heard the screams. Someone was frantically calling to her for help. She covered her ears and shut her eyes tight.

When she opened them, she was in her room, in her nightgown, safe in her bed.

How did she get here? Was this a dream too?

The room began to spin. "What is real?" Mayra asked aloud.

The awful night of horrors—was she remembering it now, or was it, too, a dream? Did it really happen?

"Begin at the beginning," she told herself, trying to get her thoughts in order, trying to slow her racing heart, trying to stop the room from spinning.

She sank back onto her pillow, closed her eyes, and tried to re-create that Saturday night. Walker. Where had she met Walker? She thought hard.

It was at the Division Street Mall. They were going to go to a movie. It was only their third or fourth date together. Walker, she remembered, was in a strange mood.

Earlier that day some kids had called him a nerd. They made fun of a magic trick he was trying to show them. Mayra told him to forget about it, but he couldn't seem to shake it off. "It's not so easy being different in Shadyside," he had said bitterly. "Everyone expects you to act like everyone else. People give me a hard time just because I'm interested in magic instead of heavy-metal groups and partying."

"Let's go to the movie," Mayra had said.

But Walker refused. "I have a better idea." His cheeks were bright red. His eyes were wild. He was talking very rapidly. He was walking so fast, she had to hurry to keep up with him.

"Walker—slow down. What are you going to do?" She began to feel nervous. She really didn't know him that well. He had never acted like this before.

She followed him to one of the mall parking lots. He began looking into cars. "Here's one," he said, after inspecting several rows. "The key is in the ignition. Get in."

It was a new-model Oldsmobile. Fire-engine red. Was he really going to steal it? "Walker—no."

He laughed. "I'm putting you on, Mayra."

"What do you mean?"

"This is my mom's car. I was just playing a joke. Come on. Get in."

"You really had me worried," she said, laughing. "You were acting so strange. I thought you were stealing it." She climbed into the front seat.

"I'm a good actor," he said, sliding behind the wheel. He moved the seat back. He had such long legs. "Magicians have to be good actors."

He backed the car out of the parking spot and headed to the exit. "Buckle up," he said. "I feel like driving fast."

"Where are we going?" she asked as he made a wide turn onto Division Street, the tires squealing.

"Don't know. Just driving." He zoomed forward through a red light. The wild look was back in his eyes.

"Wait a minute," Mayra said suspiciously. "This is your mom's car? You drove it to the mall?"

"Yeah."

"Then how come you had to move the seat back?"

He laughed. It was a laugh she hadn't heard before, a frightening laugh. She didn't like it at all.

"Okay, okay. So we're borrowing the car for a while."

"Walker—let me out!"

"I'll return it to the lot. I promise."

"Walker—how could you—"

He shrugged. "Just felt like it. Don't you ever do anything on impulse?"

He squealed around a corner, nearly colliding with a taxi. The taxi driver angrily blew his horn. Walker sped up. "Wow! This car can move. Must be a V-six."

"Walker—"

"I know, I know. I promise. A quick spin and we'll take it right back to the parking lot."

"Spin is right. Why are you driving so fast?"

He didn't answer. He had just run another red light. "Oops. Didn't see that one."

A few minutes later they were speeding up to River Ridge on a narrow, winding road that overlooked the Conononka River. River Ridge was the major makeout spot for kids from Shadyside High.

"Let's see what's happening up here tonight," Walker said.

"Slow down!" she cried.

But her warning was too late.

First she saw the headlights coming around the curve in the road. Then she saw the little yellow car. Walker swerved, but not in time.

It seemed to be happening in slow motion. Mayra

could see what was going to happen, but there was nothing she could do to stop it. She couldn't even raise her arms in time to shield her eyes. The red Oldsmobile plowed into the driver's side of the yellow car. The crash was deafening, like a bomb exploding.

She felt a hard jolt, then a softer one.

And then she heard the screams. Hideous, high-pitched screams of terror coming from the other car. Screams she would hear again and again.

She watched helplessly as the yellow car toppled over the edge of the road.

"No! Walker! No!" She was screaming without realizing it.

The Oldsmobile finally shuddered to a stop. Mayra sat frozen for a brief moment and realized she was okay. Then she leapt out of the car and ran to the side of the ridge.

Down below, the yellow car was sinking quickly into the river, making large bubbles as it submerged. "Walker—we've got to help!" Mayra cried. "Walker!"

Where was he? She turned back to see him sitting behind the wheel, motioning for her to get back in the car.

"Walker—hurry! There were at least two people in that car!"

Where were they? Why didn't they come swimming to the top?

"Walker—we've got to help them! They'll drown!"

With a loud sucking sound, the top of the car disappeared under the water.

Mayra stared down from the ridge, frozen in panic. Come up. Come up. *Please* come up.

Finally a man floated up from the sunken car.

Okay. There's one, she thought. Maybe they'll all be okay.

Splashing hard, the man started swimming to shore. A few seconds later he climbed onto the ground. Coughing and sputtering, he looked up to the top of the ridge—and saw Mayra.

"Walker—come quick!" Mayra screamed. "Get out of the car! That man—he's calling up to me, but I can't hear him!"

The man down on the river shore had signaled frantically to her, then jumped back into the water, probably to try to rescue whoever else was in the car.

"Walker—we've got to get help! Walker—"

Suddenly he was by her side. But instead of looking down to the water, he grabbed her arm and started to pull her back to the car.

"Walker—what are you doing?"

He didn't reply. He tightened his grip on her arm.

"Ow! You're *hurting* me!"

Ignoring her cries, he shoved her into the car. The next thing she knew, they were speeding away.

And then . . .

And then what?

Lying on her pillow, her eyes shut tight, Mayra dug deeply into her memory. Then what happened? She remembered she was crying. Crying and protesting. Pleading with Walker to go back.

Then what? What did we do?

Why haven't I remembered any of this till tonight?

The questions bombarded her. But in a strange way, Mayra felt relieved. Now she knew why she was sleepwalking toward water. Now she knew what had been upsetting her, what her subconscious mind was trying to deal with while she was asleep.

And now she thought she had figured out why that horrible night had escaped from her memory for so many weeks.

She thought she had it all figured out.

She just had to prove it.

Clicking on the bed-table lamp, she reached for her phone. It was late—nearly midnight—but so what?

She pushed Walker's number. It rang once, twice.

He picked it up and said hello, sounding sleepy.

When she asked him to meet her at Mrs. Cottler's house the next morning, he sounded surprised. "Uh—I can't tomorrow. How about—"

"How about tomorrow evening, then? I've got something really important to tell you."

He quickly agreed.

chapter

21

Walker took her hand and pulled her down beside him on the grassy shore. He pulled her head down to him and started to kiss her.

"No," she said, pushing him away. She sat up beside him and stared out at the gray lake.

It was a cool evening. The air felt more like autumn than summer. The trees and shrubs had faded to evening shades of gray, their shadows darkening over the ground. Far out in the lake, almost to Fear Island, two birds swooped and dived, fishing for a late supper, as wisps of fog blew over the shore.

Mayra had taken a long nap that afternoon. She had slept well for the first time in weeks. But she didn't feel at all refreshed when she awoke. She had pulled on a pair of faded, tight-legged jeans and a green- and white-striped rugby shirt, and hurried over to Mrs. Cottler's.

She had found Hazel waiting for her by the door. By

the time she had fed the cat and watered all of Mrs. Cottler's plants, Walker was knocking on the back door. He was wearing rumpled chinos and a gray sweatshirt. His hair wasn't combed.

He started to come in, but Mayra stepped outside and pulled the door shut behind her. "Such a nice, cool night. Let's go down to the lake," she had said.

Looking more than a little confused, Walker followed her down the grassy slope to the dark, silent lake.

Now Mayra sat beside him, staring down at him as he lay on his back in the tall grass. She had rehearsed all day what she wanted to say to him. But now none of it seemed right.

"What's wrong?" he asked, still holding her hand. "You look so upset. Did you sleepwalk again?"

"No," she said, and again let her eyes trail out to the lake where Fear Island had now completely disappeared in fog.

"Did you get any sleep?" Walker asked, looking concerned.

"No. I just can't sleep," she lied. "I'm too afraid to go to sleep."

"Because of the sleepwalking?"

"Yes. Every time I start to drift off, I force myself to wake up. I-I'm afraid every night. I'm just totally wrecked, Walker. I really need your help."

He sat up, still holding her hand. "My help?"

"Yes. I need you to help me calm down."

He let go of her hand. "You mean—"

"I need you to hypnotize me to calm me down. Remember you once offered to do it?"

"Well, yes. I guess I could. I don't know." He slicked back his blond hair with both hands. "I have been practicing."

"It isn't dangerous, is it?" Mayra asked, biting her lower lip.

"No, not at all. I'm really pretty good at it. I hypnotized my cousin Alice a few months ago and got her to quit smoking. It shouldn't be too hard to use a hypnotic suggestion to make you feel less anxious."

"Well, I'm desperate enough to try it, Walker. I really am," Mayra said. "I thought of it last night just before I called you. I remembered you offered once to hypnotize me and—"

"Well, it's very simple, really." He reached into his pants pocket and pulled out a pocket lighter. "First I'm going to make you feel very sleepy."

"That's what it feels like?"

"Yeah. You'll just feel like you're drifting off to sleep."

"That'll be nice," Mayra said wistfully. "It's been so long. Ever since I started working for Mrs. Cottler . . ."

"She gets back in a day or so, right?"

"Right."

"We've got to get you away from her," Walker said heatedly. "This spell she's cast on you—hey—I hope you don't think I can use hypnosis to get rid of the sleepwalking spell."

"No. Of course not," Mayra said, nervously pulling up a clump of grass and letting the moist green blades slip through her fingers. "I just want you to make me feel calmer. That's all."

"Okay," he said, giving her a reassuring smile. "In a few minutes I think you'll feel much better, Mayra. First, I want you to relax all of your muscles. That's it. Even more. Even more relaxed."

Mayra relaxed her neck muscles and her head slumped forward.

Walker clicked the lighter. It sparked, then flamed red orange. "Now I want you to follow the flame from this lighter," Walker said. "You've probably seen this done on TV and stuff. But it really works. Now, clear your mind, okay? Try not to think of anything but the flame. Concentrate on the flame. Concentrate all of your attention on the flame. Follow it. That's it. Follow it this way—then this way."

Mayra's eyes followed the lighter from side to side, up and down. Her eyelids started to droop.

"You're starting to feel sleepy. That's good. Let yourself go," Walker said in a whisper. "You're going to close your eyes now. It's going to feel so good to close your eyes. Go ahead. Go to sleep. Close your eyes. And when you open them, you will feel very calm, very rested, very peaceful."

Mayra closed her eyes. Walker continued whispering for a long while. Mayra nodded her head in response. But she didn't open her eyes. Her arms hung perfectly still at her sides.

"In a few moments I'm going to tell you to open your eyes," Walker said softly. "And when you open your eyes, you will feel very rested. You will feel as if you've had the best night's sleep of your life. And you will feel completely at peace with yourself. The anxieties that were upsetting you will be forgotten. You will feel completely calm."

Mayra, her eyelids lightly closed, nodded slowly, peacefully.

"And when you open your eyes," Walker said, still speaking very softly, "you will continue to forget about that night on River Ridge. You will not be troubled by the yellow car. You will have no memory of the accident, no memory of the yellow car, no memory of going to River Ridge with me. When you open your eyes—"

Mayra opened her eyes and her entire body tensed. She leapt to her feet and grabbed the front of Walker's sweatshirt with both hands.

"You filthy creep!" she screamed. "I *knew* that's what you did to me that horrible night! My sleepwalking—it was all your fault—and you've known it all along!"

chapter

22

Walker's mouth dropped open in surprise and the two pink spots on his cheeks turned scarlet. He started to climb to his feet, but Mayra shoved him back down. She stood over him, glaring in fury.

"I take it you were only pretending to be hypnotized right now," he said, his voice breaking.

"That's right. I wanted to be awake, to hear what you had to say."

"It was all a trap."

"You catch on quickly. You had no business to do that to me, Walker, to hypnotize me that night and make me forget about the accident. You had no right to mess with my mind like that."

"You were going to tell the police," he said coldly. "I couldn't let you do that. I couldn't let you ruin both of our lives because of a stupid accident."

"A stupid accident? People might have died in that car, Walker! We don't even know how many people were in the car, do we? Because you ran away. You didn't do anything to help. You let people die."

"One person," he said, looking away. "One man died. I read it in the paper. The other guy, his brother, lived."

"But I didn't read it in the paper, did I?" she said bitterly, kicking a clump of grass at him. "Because I didn't even remember I was there. You saw to that, didn't you!"

"I had to. I have an exciting life ahead of me. I can't have it ruined by one stupid mistake."

"A stupid mistake? You're a hit-and-run killer, Walker!" Mayra screamed. She knew she was out of control now, but she couldn't stop herself. "And all this time you knew why I was sleepwalking. You knew what was troubling me, why I was sleepwalking to water. I couldn't deal with it consciously because of what you did when you hypnotized me that night."

"I just hypnotized you to calm you down. You even agreed to it," Walker said, still not looking her in the eye. "Then, when I had you hypnotized, I decided to—uh—well . . ."

"And you let me go along all these weeks thinking that some poor, innocent old woman had cast a spell on me—just because it got you off the hook!"

Walker stared out at the lake and didn't reply.

"You don't care about me at all, do you? *Do* you?" Mayra demanded.

Walker jumped to his feet and took a few steps away from her. "I've been going out with Suki," he said. "Everybody in the world knows that. I just hung around you to make sure your memory didn't come back."

Mayra made two fists. She wanted to pound Walker into dust, but she forced her hands to stay at her sides. "I've got bad news for you, Walker," she said through clenched teeth. "My memory is back. All of it. And I'm going to call the police right now."

"No, you're not." He had that wild look in his eyes again, the same expression he'd had the night he'd stolen the car, the night of the accident.

Suddenly he moved forward and wrapped his arms around her waist, trapping her hands at her sides. "Hey—let go!" she screamed. He was stronger than she'd imagined.

He lifted her over his shoulder and carried her toward the lake. "Put me down! What are you going to do?"

"I can't let you call the police," he said, speaking very calmly, too calmly. "I can't let you ruin my life. I'm going to be a famous magician. I can't let you ruin that."

She struggled to get away, but his grip was iron tight. He dropped her off the small dock into the water, bent down, grabbed her head and neck, and shoved her face down beneath the surface.

She struggled to the top, gasping for air. "Walker, please—"

"I'm sorry," he said, still sounding so eerily calm. "You should've let me hypnotize you. It would've been so much easier."

"You're really going to drown me?" she screamed.

He didn't reply. Instead, he pushed her head back under the water and held it there.

chapter
23

Mayra kicked her legs, trying to free herself. But he stayed at the edge of the dock, holding her head, pushing her down. She tried turning onto her side, thinking maybe she could slip away. But he held her too tightly.

Her lungs were about to burst.

I'm drowning in this lake for the second time, she thought.

Then his grip loosened.

She heard him cry out.

She raised her head and sucked in a mouthful of air.

What was going on? He had let go of her entirely. She rolled away, stumbled on the wet lake shore, regained her feet.

Walker was struggling with something.

She brushed her wet hair away from her eyes. She took a deep breath, then another.

Hazel!

The black cat was standing on Walker's shoulder, screeching loudly and clawing at his face and neck. "Get off! Get off me!" Walker howled.

How did Hazel get out here? Mayra wondered. Did she sneak out when I left with Walker?

Struggling to rid himself of the clawing cat, Walker fell over backward.

Mayra didn't wait around to see what happened next. This was her only chance to escape. Feeling heavy and weighted down by her wet clothes, she started to run over the tall grass.

Her wet sneakers slipped on the grass. She fell, but quickly picked herself up. Running as fast as she could, Mayra felt around in her jeans pocket for Mrs. Cottler's keys.

Did she have them?

She had to get inside the house. She had to call the police.

The keys. The keys. Where were they?

Yes! She felt them in her other pocket.

It seemed like hours, but it was less than a minute later that she was struggling with the back door lock. Then she was inside the house, breathing hard, her heart pounding. She locked the door behind her and listened.

She couldn't hear Walker or the cat from here.

The phone. She hurried to the kitchen phone and, pushing her long, wet hair from her face, dialed 911.

She was totally out of breath and had to repeat everything at least twice, but she was pretty sure she'd gotten her message across to the voice on the other end. The police were on their way.

Feeling a little relieved, Mayra slumped against the kitchen counter.

"Hey!"

Hazel was lying on the small rug in front of the sink, licking her left paw.

"How'd you get back here so quickly?"

How strange. Less than two minutes before, the cat had been down by the lake. How did she get back in the house? It looked as if she had been in this spot for quite a while.

Mayra didn't have long to think about the cat. She cried out as a rock flew into the kitchen, shattering the window. "No!" she cried, backing away.

chapter

24

Mayra stared in horror as one leg appeared over the window ledge, pushing out the remaining shards of glass. Then the other leg swung into the kitchen. Walker, blood pouring from long scratch marks down his face, stepped into the room.

He wiped blood off his cheek with the sleeve of his sweatshirt and glared at Mayra. "You won't get away this time."

"Walker, you're too late. I already called the police."

He stood by the wall, breathing hard. He took a step toward her, his sneakers crunching over broken window glass.

Blood from the cat scratches poured down his cheeks in dark rivulets. His eyes were wild. "You shouldn't have done that."

He took another step toward her.

"You're bleeding," Mayra said.

153

He wiped his face again with the already-bloodstained sleeve of his sweatshirt. "You shouldn't have," he repeated, moving closer.

"Don't take another step," she warned. She looked for a weapon, something she could use to defend herself. "Let me wash off your face for you." Maybe she could stall him by being nice to him.

"You'll ruin our lives," he said.

"Walker, I said let me help you clean out those scratches."

He didn't seem to hear her. He took another step toward her.

Hazel stood up suddenly, eyeing Walker warily. She tilted her head and meowed a loud warning, her lips pulled back over her teeth.

"I can't let you ruin our lives," Walker repeated.

Behind him, Mayra saw Mrs. Cottler's big meat cleaver, resting on the counter near the sink.

Chop, chop, chop.

She heard the sound again of Mrs. Cottler chopping away.

Why had the cleaver been left out like that? It was almost as if it had been left there for Mayra to use.

"Stay back, Walker," she said.

He took another step across the kitchen.

I have to protect myself, she thought. He's really out of his head. He already tried to kill me once.

But how can I get the cleaver? I'd have to walk past him.

Then, with a loud groan, he lunged toward her. She swerved out of his grasp, ducked under him, her arm outstretched. He turned, surprised, in time to see her grab up the heavy cleaver.

For some reason he grinned.

Again he wiped the blood from his face with the sleeve of his sweatshirt. He was breathing even more heavily now, wheezing as he breathed. "What are you going to do with that, Mayra?"

She raised it in front of her, surprised by how much it weighed. "Just stay back," she said, her voice shaking.

"What are you going to do with that?" he repeated, moving toward her.

"I'm serious, Walker. Stay back." She raised the cleaver higher.

"What are you going to do with that?"

He ran at her, startling her.

She knew she couldn't use the cleaver.

"What are you going to do with that?" he screamed.

He grabbed for it, tried to pull it from her hands. They wrestled for control of it, their arms over their heads.

"No!" Mayra screamed. "Get off! No!"

He was so surprisingly strong. She couldn't hold on to it any longer. He pulled the cleaver away from her.

"No!" she screamed, her throat choked with terror.

She shoved him hard in the stomach and took off, running out of the kitchen, through the hallway to the front door. She could hear him right behind her.

"No!"

She had to get out of there.

She pulled open the door.

And screamed.

Cal was standing in the doorway. He stared at her, grim-faced, seething with anger. He was wearing baggy jeans and a faded denim jacket, and carrying a large wooden cane. Behind him on the street she saw a red pickup truck parked at the curb.

Cal's red pickup truck.

He was the one, the one who drove Donna off the road.

I'm surrounded, she thought.

I'm lost.

chapter

25

Cal glared at her, his face bright red. His body was tensed, his legs spread apart as if expecting trouble.

"Who are you? What do you want?" Mayra cried.

Walker, approaching from behind, stopped short when he saw the look on Cal's face.

"Who *are* you? What do you want? Say something!" Mayra screamed.

But to her surprise Cal pushed past her to get to Walker. "You killed my brother!" he screamed.

Walker gasped and started to raise the meat cleaver.

Cal moved quickly. He swung the cane hard, and the cleaver flew from Walker's hand. Then Cal tackled Walker, pushing him over backward onto the hallway carpet, and pinned him down, pressing the cane against Walker's chest.

"You killed my brother," he repeated.

"Stop. I—I can't breathe," Walker groaned.

Cal ignored him. His powerful muscles bulged as he kept Walker pinned down with the cane. He looked up at Mayra, who was still frozen in shock at the doorway.

"Don't kill him!" Mayra cried as Cal pressed the cane down against Walker's throat. "Don't kill him—please!"

"All along I thought it was you," Cal said, breathing heavily, ignoring her pleas. "Then tonight I was up here by the house. I heard you shouting down at the lake, and I knew the truth. I knew *he* was the one who killed my brother and drove off. I heard everything you said. Then I saw him try to drown you. I started to come help you. But I can't move very well with this cane—especially on grass. Luckily, you got away."

"Please—let me up," Walker said, choking. "I won't do anything. I swear."

Cal ignored him.

"You mean you—" Mayra started.

But she stopped because she heard a noise at the front door. She spun around to see two solemn-faced policemen. They both had their hands in readiness on their gun holsters. One of them pulled open the screen door, and they both stepped inside.

"What exactly is going on here?" one of them asked.

Cal quickly let go of Walker and stood up, leaning heavily on the wooden cane. Walker made no move to get up. The policemen bent over him. "You okay, kid?"

"You were in the yellow car?" Mayra asked Cal,

relieved that she was safe, eager to hear the rest of the story.

"My brother Jerry and I were in the car," Cal said, talking rapidly, still out of breath. "I saw you up on the ridge. I thought you were the driver. I thought you were going to help me save Jerry. But then you just drove away."

"I wanted to help," Mayra said. "Walker pulled me away."

"My brother drowned. Afterward, I guess I went a little crazy. I had your face in my mind. I couldn't forget your face. I thought you killed my brother, so I wanted to find you."

"I'm so sorry," Mayra said.

The two policemen looked at each other, not understanding a word of this.

"Then I came out of my house and bumped into you outside the old lady's house on Fear Street," Cal continued. "I couldn't believe I'd actually found you. I've known Mrs. Cottler for years, so when I made up a story about wanting you to baby-sit for my niece, she gave me your address, no problem."

"And then you tried to kill me with your pickup truck?" Mayra asked, suddenly feeling weak, leaning against the banister for support.

"I thought it was you in the car. I only wanted to scare you," Cal said. "But it was so wet and slippery, I lost control. I didn't mean to crack us both up. I ended up in the hospital with a wrecked ankle and a wrecked knee. That's why I've got this cane."

"Oh, good lord. When I saw you there, I thought you were a mental patient!" Mayra cried.

"Maybe I should be," Cal said grimly. "I can't believe I had the wrong person the whole time. It-it's been so bad for me—since Jerry died."

"Will you stop yakking and tell us what exactly is going on here?" one of the policemen demanded impatiently.

"It's sort of a long story," Mayra told him.

chapter

26

One Week Later

"*I* admit it. I've been a real creep."

"I'll second that motion," Mayra said.

Link gave her his hurt look. "I didn't mean to be a creep," he said quietly.

"No creep ever does," Mayra said playfully.

"The only reason I was such a creep was that I cared about you so much."

Mayra laughed. "So let me get this straight. It was *my* fault that you acted like a creep."

"Right," Link agreed quickly. He scooted closer to her on the couch and put his arm around her shoulders.

"That's so like you," Mayra said.

"What? I didn't hear you. Did you say, 'I like you'?"

"No. How can I like you? You're a creep. An admitted creep."

He pulled her face to his and kissed her, holding her cheeks gently with his warm hands.

"Well, maybe I like you a little," she said thoughtfully.

He kissed her again, longer this time.

"Maybe I just like creeps," Mayra admitted. She looked at her watch. "Hey—I don't have time for this. I've got to get to Mrs. Cottler's house. She's back. She said I could come and pick up my paycheck."

"Paycheck? Great! Then you can treat me to lunch!" Link got up and followed her out of the den. "Come on. I'll drive you to Aunt Lucy's." They walked out the front door. Link started jogging toward the red pickup truck in the drive.

Seeing the red truck made Mayra stop. "You must've thought I was a real jerk, thinking it was you who tried to run me down."

"No, not at all," he said, taking her hand and pulling her to the truck. "I'm a creep, remember? A creep can't call a jerk a jerk. It's not allowed."

"But Stephanie must think I'm totally bananas. I mean, I practically accused her of being a witch!"

"I explained everything to Stephanie," Link said, holding open the truck door for her.

"And?"

"And you're right. She thinks you're totally bananas!" He laughed and slammed the truck door.

He's so great looking when he laughs like that, Mayra thought.

"Stephanie's eager to make up with you," Link said, starting up the truck and backing down the drive.

"She *was* casting a spell or something when I burst into her room that day," Mayra said defensively.

"Well, she and I are both interested in the occult," Link said. "I guess because of Aunt Lucy."

"Mrs. Cottler is really a witch?"

Link's mouth dropped open. "Huh?" He stared at her.

"Watch the road," she warned.

"Aunt Lucy a witch? Are you kidding? She's a really well-known professor. She has a Ph.D. She taught occult studies at several universities until she retired a few years ago. She's published about a dozen books on the subject!"

Mayra had to laugh. "I guess I got that a little wrong. Maybe I'm still sleepwalking!"

A few minutes later they were greeted by Mrs. Cottler, who seemed very pleased to see them both. "I won't keep you youngsters," Mrs. Cottler said cheerily. "It's such a beautiful Saturday. You don't want to spend it with a tiresome old lady."

She handed Mayra her paycheck. "Oh. I almost forgot, dear. I have something else for you."

She disappeared into the other room, leaning on her cane. A few minutes later she returned, carrying a box that she handed to Mayra. "Here are your beads. All restrung. I did it while I was up at my sister's. Sorry it took so long. I hope you didn't think I'd run off with them!"

Mayra held up the beads and admired them. "What a beautiful job. Thank you!" She put them around her neck.

"You're a very good reader, Mayra," Mrs. Cottler said. "I can't wait till Monday. Maybe we'll start a new book."

"That sounds like fun," Mayra said. "Sound like a good idea to *you*, Hazel?"

Mayra looked down at the cat, who was sunning herself in front of the kitchen window.

That strange cat, Mayra thought.

How *did* she get down to the lake to rescue me from Walker? And how did she get back to the house before I did?

She stared at Hazel. The cat tilted her head and stared back at Mayra.

I guess that's one mystery that just won't be cleared up, Mayra thought. And she followed Link out the door onto Fear Street.

About the Author

R. L. STINE is the author of more than 70 books of humor, adventure, and mystery for young readers. In recent years, he has been concentrating on scary thrillers such as this one.

For ten years, he was editor of *Bananas,* a national humor magazine for young people. In addition to magazine and book writing, he is currently Head Writer of the children's TV show "Eureeka's Castle."

He lives in New York City with his wife Jane and son Matt.

THE NIGHTMARES
NEVER END . . .
WHEN YOU VISIT

NEXT: *HAUNTED*

The ghost of Paul Starett has come back
to Fear Street to haunt Melissa Dryden.
"I don't remember how I died,"
he tells her. "I only know that
you were responsible!"

Melissa knows that she didn't kill Paul.
But how can she prove it to the ghost
before he seeks his deadly revenge?